Santa Fe Assassin
A Fernando Lopez Santa Fe Mystery

Santa Fe Assassin

A Fernando Lopez Santa Fe Mystery

James C. Wilson

Santa Fe

© 2024 by James C. Wilson
All Rights Reserved
No part of this book may be reproduced in any form or by any electronic or mechanical means including information storage and retrieval systems without permission in writing from the publisher, except by a reviewer who may quote brief passages in a review.

Sunstone books may be purchased for educational, business, or sales promotional use. For information please write: Special Markets Department, Sunstone Press, P.O. Box 2321, Santa Fe, New Mexico 87504-2321.
Printed on acid-free paper
∞
eBook: 978-1-61139-751-2

LIBRARY OF CONGRESS CATALOGING IN PUBLICATION DATA (ON FILE)

WWW.SUNSTONEPRESS.COM
SUNSTONE PRESS / POST OFFICE BOX 2321 / SANTA FE, NM 87504-2321 /USA
(505) 988-4418

I had not thought death had undone so many.
—T.S. Eliot, *The Waste Land*

Ambush

Andy Dejon saw the trouble as he approached Nageezi, the snarl of cars and pickups scattered along Highway 550. More vehicles packed the parking lot where Navajo artists usually sold their jewelry and pottery from the back of their trucks. Beyond the parking lot a group of rowdies had closed County Road 7900 to Chaco Canyon and the ruins of its ancient stone city. The troublemakers shouted and gestured angrily at the coalition of environmental groups who had gathered to celebrate the establishment of a ten-mile buffer zone preventing oil drilling around Chaco Culture National Historical Park in order to protect its fragile ruins. Interior Secretary Dee Highland was supposed to address the crowd later today.

Andy pulled off the highway. He drove over loose gravel into the ditch behind a massive Ford F-350 pickup with Arizona license plates. The Arizona plates told him some of the protesters were outsiders. That made sense, because why would any New Mexican object to protecting Chaco, a one-thousand-year-old city that became a World Heritage Site in 1987? Especially this late in the game, after all the work the environmental coalition had done to get the ten-mile buffer zone approved. Didn't make sense to him. He wished he'd arrived earlier. Stopping for coffee and a snack at the McDonald's in Cuba had been a big mistake. Now he didn't see how he could get into the park.

As soon as he stepped out of his Subaru Outback Andy heard a bullhorn blasting its amplified messages: "Go home! No Trespassing! Stay off Allottee Land!"

"Allottee" meaning individual Navajos who lived in the area on a piece of land allotted to them by the government. The allottees were allowed to graze their sheep on the land surrounding the national park.

From the road Andy thought he recognized some of the coalition people trying to enter the park. Members of Save Chaco Now, Environment America, the New Mexico Wildlife Federation, and even the All Pueblo

Council of Governors. He did not see any government vehicles, which meant that Secretary Highland had not yet arrived. Maybe she'd cancelled her appearance because of the trouble. Highland and other officials were supposed to address the crowd of environmentalists coming to celebrate the occasion. Now what?

Gravel crunched under his feet as he walked to the County Road leading into Chaco. The morning was fresh and clear, a typical New Mexico morning with a deep blue sky and plenty of sunshine. Too bad this had to happen. It would have been spectacular to hold the festivities in the ancient stone city considered the ancestral homeland of the Pueblo people. A damn shame for the Pueblos and the environmental community.

The noise level increased in intensity as he walked down the county road. Both sides shouted angrily at each other. Small skirmishes broke out everywhere, with people pushing and shoving and fighting over signs. When some of the signs were ripped down, the protesters began using them as clubs, smacking the celebrants trying to get into the park. Up ahead he thought he saw George Ortiz, one of the other coordinators of the Save Chaco Now group. He waved, trying to get George's attention. George raised his fist high above his head to acknowledge Andy. Maybe the two of them could at least try to speak to the protesters and somehow stop the confrontation before someone got badly hurt. Or even worse.

"Go home!" an angry protester yelled and shoved him as he struggled to enter the crowded parking lot. Let it go, he told himself. Striking back would just make the situation worse. Jostled by the angry mob, he noticed the rowdies protesting the event were about half Anglo and half Native American, almost certainly Navajo allottees wanting to use the land as they saw fit.

It crossed his mind that he was fortunate his wife Tessa had refused to come with him, even though she too belonged to the Save Chaco Now group. He was in the proverbial doghouse again because he didn't share her definition of marriage as monogamous. She'd told him to go fuck himself when he asked if she wanted to come today. Turned out to be for the best, because Tessa had a hot temper and would have charged right up to the protesters and given them a piece of her mind. No doubt she would have been one of the first casualties, he thought, watching one protester clobber an elderly man wearing a Sierra Club T-shirt. The old man staggered backwards, with his straw hat smashed flat on his head.

When George turned his way, Andy raised his hand again and called out. He lunged forward, trying to force his way through the crowd. Just then he heard two muffled pops.

Thok! Thok!

The bullets staggered him. What the fuck? It felt like someone had punched him in the back, twice.

The woman next to him screamed and covered her face.

Andy opened his mouth to speak but nothing came out. Instead, he staggered a few steps and sank to his knees. Then he collapsed face down in the sand.

1

Private Investigator Fernando Lopez sat in his office brooding about retirement. He'd already made the decision to retire, and yet every morning he found himself driving down to his office on Canyon Road at the usual time, around ten o'clock. This morning he was making a list of things he needed to do before officially retiring: pack up his office files, remove his Private Eye sign out front, and drink up what Modelo remained in the mini-fridge he kept in his office. That sounded easy enough, especially the Modelo, but then again he kept thinking about what his friend and nominal landlord Ruby Montez said. She told him to leave everything in his office just as it was in case he couldn't stand being retired and decided to un-retire. On the other hand his wife Estelle, who didn't like Ruby, wanted him to retire immediately. So what to do?

One thing for sure, he hadn't had much business lately. His last paying customer was a mother who's sixteen-year-old son had gone missing. Fernando found the lad living in an ashram up in Taos, still the land of ashrams and communes. Turned out the mother knew the whereabouts of her son all along. What she really wanted was for Fernando to kidnap the kid and bring him home against his will. As if! The woman refused to pay him for the longest time but finally paid half of his fee because, she said, the job was half done. Otherwise, most of his messages over the past month had been crank calls: missing animals and UFOs and other such nonsense.

Fernando stared at the meager notes he'd made on his legal pad. He checked his watch. Eleven o'clock. In another half hour he could go next door to Ruby's gallery and see if she wanted to go for lunch at El Farol. A potter by trade, Ruby owned a pottery co-op in the Railyard District and the gallery next door, which she'd inherited from her ex-husband Jimmy Mackey who was murdered in Taos (not in an ashram or commune!). He and Ruby and several other Canyon Road artists spent a lot of time–and money–at El Farol, especially come Happy Hour every afternoon about four o'clock.

Thinking about lunch, Fernando heard footsteps coming down the gravel path to his door. Then two shadows appeared outside the window, one considerably larger than the other. The door opened and Manny Alvarez stepped inside. A small dapper man in his forties, Manny had replaced Fernando as Chief Detective at the Santa Fe Police Department. Sargent Antonio Blake followed, a huge ex-Marine who stood six feet, eight inches tall and weighed close to two hundred and eighty pounds. Down at the Washington Avenue Station Antonio was known as the enforcer, since no one ever wanted to tangle with the big man.

Manny saluted and cracked a joke, as he usually did. A real smart-ass. "You know, for a retired man, you sure spend a lot of time in your office."

Fernando laughed. "I can't stay away. After I finish my coffee and read the newspaper every morning, I drive down here automatically. It's like sleepwalking. I have no choice in the matter."

"Have you read this morning's *Independent*?" Manny asked.

Fernando nodded, frowning. Why all the questions?

"Then you know about the shooting at Nageezi," Manny said.

"Chaco Canyon? Yeah, I read the story," Fernando said.

"Do you know Andy Dejon, the man who was killed?" Manny asked.

Fernando shook his head. "Just his name from the Save Chaco Now group. I think he was one of the officers."

"Well, he's married to Tessa Montez, Ruby's sister," Manny said, walking over and sitting in one of the chairs facing Fernando's desk. Antonio followed, taking the other chair.

Fernando looked from one to the other. "So that's why you're here?"

"Maybe, but it's more than that. We have a tricky situation on our hands," Antonio said.

Fernando waited. "I'm listening."

Manny sighed. "Chief got a notice from the FBI that Jack Lacy is in town. The Feds keep a close watch on Lacy's whereabouts. Do you know who Jack Lacy is?"

Fernando shook his head. "Never heard of him."

"He's a professional hit man," Antonio said, taking over from Manny. "He usually works in the Mideast or sometimes Eastern Europe. The last I heard he was in Berlin."

"Wait…you know this guy?" Fernando asked.

Antonio nodded. "He's an ex-Marine from my company. I knew him as Sargent Jack Lacy. He was the highest rated Scout Sniper in the Marines back then. We called him the Grim Reaper. Thing is, he never deployed. I mean he left the service, but he kept on killing. For money, lots of money.

He charges hundreds of thousands of dollars to assassinate politicians and wealthy business types. People the international moneyed interests want removed. Or neutralized, I think that's the language they use."

"And you think this Jack Lacy killed Andy Dejon at Nageezi?" Fernando asked, starting to understand why they'd come.

"We don't know anything at this point," Manny replied. "We don't know why Lacy's here or who hired him, if anyone. Same with Dejon's murder. We don't know if it was Lacy who shot him or someone else."

"Maybe it's just a coincidence, maybe Lacy's on vacation in Old Santa Fe," Fernando said, smiling.

Both Manny and Antonio stared at him, not smiling.

"We think Lacy's staying at La Fonda under the name of Jack Green," Antonio said. "I'm thinking of paying him a visit, trying to find out for myself. We used to be friends, or at least friendly."

Manny shook his head. "Yeah, I don't know if that's such a good idea."

Antonio turned to Manny. "Do you have a better idea?"

The question lingered in the air.

Finally Fernando broke the silence. "So what do you want from me? Why are you telling me this?"

"We may need your advice...or your help," Manny said. "You know the lay of the land here better than anyone in the department, including the Chief, who's a relative newcomer."

Antonio nodded. "Yeah, because what I can't figure out is this: who in Santa Fe would have the kind of money to hire Lacy? I mean, sure, there's lots of people with money here, rich people from the coasts mostly, but I can't think of anyone who would be able and willing to offer a half-million dollar bounty on someone in Santa Fe."

"Exactly," Manny said. "Unless it would be Silva Archivada, the reported head of the Sinaloa Cartel in the Southwest."

That seemed far-fetched to Fernando. "I doubt that. Sure, he would have the money, but why would be want to assassinate a no-name local like Andy Dejon?" Fernando asked.

Manny shook his head.

"Forget about Dejon for a minute," Antonio added. "Maybe Silva Archivada is who Lacy's supposed to assassinate. That makes more sense. I mean, who else in Sana Fe would be worth a million dollars to knock off?"

Fernando laughed. "Good point."

"Anyway, that's why we wanted to talk with you, given the possible involvement of the Sinaloa Cartel," Antonio said.

Manny agreed. "I mean, we hope the cartel's not involved. I don't have any desire to get involved with those bastards again. They cost me a kidney and six weeks in the hospital. But...."

"Thanks for the invitation," Fernando said, not pleased with this turn of events. "What is it you want me to do?"

Neither Antonio nor Manny had an answer to that question. "Nothing at the moment," Manny said, "but we might need you later. Given your experience."

Fernando frowned. "Lucky me."

Manny stood and stretched and then turned to go. "We'll be in touch."

Antonio followed the little man but stopped at the door. "So you see...you can't retire now, even if you want to, old buddy."

2

After his office door closed Fernando listened to Manny and Antonio's footsteps walking away on the gravel path outside. He tossed his retirement list in the bottom drawer of the desk, along with all of his other discarded crap. So much for his plan. Like Manny, he had no desire to tangle with a professional assassin or the Sinaloa Cartel, but he felt an obligation to help Manny and Antonio. They had been his best friends for years. Not only that, but both of them had saved his ass on more than one occasion. He owed them. Big time.

Fernando fetched the morning newspaper out of his wastebasket and reread the front page news story about the Nageezi shooting. He didn't notice anything he'd missed the first time. Still didn't make any damn sense. Of all the people on both sides of the barricades, why Andy Dejon? Was it an indiscriminate or a targeted killing?

As far as Fernando knew, Dejon was a local yokel from Abiquiu who belonged to a no-name environmental organization. Why would anyone pay a professional assassin hundreds of thousands of dollars to kill him?

While he brooded he heard angry footsteps stomping down the gravel path to his office. What now? Suddenly the door flew open and Ruby burst into his office waving the old Glock revolver she'd inherited from her dead ex-husband.

Fernando ducked, thinking Ruby had come gunning for him for some unknown reason. Not paying his utility bills?

"What's wrong with you?" Ruby asked, glancing at Fernando crouching behind his desk. Ruby looked like she'd just come from her pottery co-op, with smudges of gray clay on her jeans and black tank top. Her long luxurious black hair was tied in a ponytail behind her head making her look ten years younger and drop dead gorgeous for a woman of her age, which also happened to be Fernando's age.

"Put the gun away!" Fernando shouted. "That looks like the gun that shot off my finer tip at El Farol, thanks to your damned ex-husband."

"I need bullets...fast!" Ruby shouted back, still waving the gun in front of her.

Fernando sat up straight in his desk chair, cautiously. "Why do you need bullets? How do you know that old gun still fires?"

"I need to shoot Bud Powers or Dick Sandoval or maybe one of the others, I don't know who exactly...."

Fernando shook his head. "Who are these people? Why do you want to shoot them?"

"I don't have time to explain now. I need bullets."

"Well, I don't have any nine millimeter cartridges, which is what that thing takes," Fernando said. "My Smith and Wesson's a forty-five."

"Shit! Maybe Blaine has some," Ruby said and ran out of the office as fast as she ran in. Just like that. Gone.

Fernando took a deep breath and tried to relax. He loved Ruby, even though she could get worked up. He and Ruby were old friends from the culture wars. Her in-your-face personality put off many people but had made her a force in Santa Fe politics for over two decades. A potter by trade, Ruby had risen through the ranks of *La Raza* to become the most progressive member of City Council ever. Back in the 1990s she fought tooth and nail with all the greedy developers who wanted to turn downtown Santa Fe into one big shopping mall. She led rallies, marches, protests, sit-ins, and if you believed the rumors, a fire-bombing or two.

She lost, of course. The developers and the Sotheby's crowd turned Santa Fe into Disneyland Southwest. The tide of gentrification sweeping over Santa Fe during those years hollowed out the city. Gone were most of the people whose families had lived in Santa Fe for generations. Ever higher home values and property taxes priced out all who couldn't afford million dollar homes. After two tumultuous terms on City Council lecturing, berating, cajoling, and threatening the other members, Ruby said 'fuck it' and retired to the pottery co-op she owned and ran with a number of other potters, all of them women.

Ruby inherited her Canyon Road studio from her ex-husband, Jimmy Mackey. Jimmy was a painter with a modest reputation in Santa Fe and northern New Mexico who was murdered in a raunchy sex scandal involving a host of Canyon Road artists as well as the then mayor of Santa Fe and his estranged wife. Fortunately for Fernando, the studio came with a detached garage that needed an occupant at about the same time he resigned as chief detective on the Santa Fe Police Department and decided to set up office as a private investigator.

The arrangement worked well for both of them. Especially for Fernando, since Ruby had never charged him rent, only utilities. He had no idea what Ruby got out of the arrangement. Security? Companionship? She liked having him next door, someone to listen to her diatribes, for sure. Must be something like that because Ruby kept trying to talk him out of retiring.

After relaxing for a few minutes, curiosity got the better of him. He didn't have anything better to do, so Fernando booted up his laptop and searched online for any mention of Jack Lacy, the professional assassin who had appeared in Santa Fe. Staying at La Fonda on the Plaza, of all places–the most public, most visible hotel in Santa Fe. He found only two references, both from the Mideast. Lacy's name surfaced on a Saudi Arabia bank's website and on the website of a holding company in Kuwait, whatever a holding company was, he had no idea. He gave up after a few minutes, convinced that Jack Lacy lived a highly secretive life. Which begged the question, why was he in Santa Fe? To shoot Andy Dejon? That struck him as absurd!

Just as he closed his laptop he heard a vehicle brake and turn into the parking lot outside. Two doors slammed. Ruby and Blaine?

He went outside to see, leaving his office door wide open. What he saw surprised him. Ruby times two: one older, one younger. The younger Ruby was thinner and had shorter, shoulder-length black hair, but otherwise the two women looked nearly identical. Like seeing double.

The older Ruby spotted Fernando coming down the gravel path. She waved. As he approached she pointed to younger Ruby. "Fernando, this is my kid sister, Tessa. I don't think you two have met. She was married to Andy Dejon, the guy who was shot and killed at Nageezi."

"The bastard!' Tessa said angrily, shocking Fernando, who expected a grieving widow.

Ruby saw Fernando's confusion. "He was a pig, a cheating no good pig!"

Tessa nodded, tears rolling down her cheeks now.

"Sorry for your loss," Fernando said, unsure of how to respond. Congratulations on your loss?

Tessa wiped away her tears.

"And sorry for your marital problems," Fernando added, feeling inadequate to the situation.

"He always said he believed in a different version of marriage," Tessa said tearfully. "Hah! His version allowed him to screw every woman who crossed his path. By now he's bedded most of the eligible women in Abiquiu and then some. I hate the bastard!"

"No kidding," Ruby said. "So why did you stay married to him? I still don't understand."

Tessa looked down, apparently embarrassed. "Well...he was good in bed!" she blurted out, laughing.

"Hah! Now you're starting to make sense," Ruby said. "It's damn hard to find a man who's good in bed or even likes sex. Trust me. I've been with a lot of men."

"Yes, you have," Fernando said without thinking.

Ruby gave him a dirty look.

"Anyway, I got the bullets from Blaine," Ruby said, pulling a box of 9 mm. cartridges out of her purse. "We're ready to hunt the bastards down, as soon as we find out which one killed Andy."

"What do you mean 'which one'?" Fernando asked. "What are you talking about?"

"Which of the husbands whose wife Andy screwed shot and killed him," Ruby said. "We've narrowed the list down to about four or five cuckolded husbands."

"Maybe just two," Tessa added. "Bud Powers or Ray Sandoval. I don't think the others cared very much. Everyone sleeps around in Abiquiu, you know. Except me. I'm a fucking idiot."

"You're not a fucking idiot, you're just busy with the gallery," Ruby said. "Somebody had to do it."

"That's right, somebody had to do it," Tessa agreed. "He was too busy cheating on me."

Ruby shook her head. "Still, we can't let some jealous asshole kill Andy and get away with it. Whoever did this will pay."

Fernando threw up his hands in desperation. "You can't just drive up to Abiquiu and start shooting jealous husbands. It's crazy, Ruby! You'll just get yourself in trouble. Take your story to the San Juan County Sheriff's Office. You could help with their investigation."

Ruby looked at him askance. "You must be kidding, Fernando. The San Juan County Sheriff's Office? Since when have they ever solved a murder case...or anything!"

That he couldn't answer.

4

Fernando woke up next morning feeling groggy. He'd spent most of the night tossing and turning, caught in a web of nightmares that, best as he could remember, involved two women shooting up a bunch of male chauvinist pigs in Bolivia a la Butch Cassidy and the Sundance Kid. Thankfully he'd woken up before Butch and Sundance, here Ruby and Tessa, ran out of the building into a hail of bullets from a pack of male chauvinist pigs wearing Bolivian Army uniforms and huge black moustaches. Scared the hell out of him.

Fernando lay in bed for several minutes realizing that he was worried about Ruby and Tessa. The only way he could assure their safety would be to go to Abiquiu with them and keep them out of trouble. Just what he wanted to do, tag along with Ruby and Tessa while they confronted jealous husbands whose wives happened to sleep with Tessa's dear, departed, cheating husband. Yes, but he couldn't let Ruby go up there waving that old pistol around, asking for trouble. Truth was, he'd always had a crush on Ruby; the two of them had known each other since high school. They'd never acted on their mutual affection, but they'd always been there for each other in times of need. Ruby probably wouldn't admit it, but she needed him now on this crazy excursion to Abiquiu.

When he felt awake enough to climb out of bed, he made his way to the kitchen and found the coffee pot empty. Estelle had already left for work at the Saint Francis Outreach Program, a nonprofit that provided foot and clothing and other necessities to the growing immigrant population coming through Santa Fe, a sanctuary city. So he brewed himself a cup of Sumatra in his Keurig and sat down at the kitchen table to read the daily newspaper.

After he finished reading the *Independent* and drinking a second cup of coffee, Fernando showered and got dressed for the day. Then, ready for action, he speed dialed Ruby on his cell phone.

"Fernando?" Ruby answered.

"I'm coming with you," Fernando said.

"Coming with me? What are you talking about?" Ruby responded, sounding half asleep even though it was nearly nine o'clock.

"I'm coming with you and Tessa to Abiquiu," Fernando said. "I want to make sure you don't get yourself in trouble or worse, shot. Going up there threatening to kill these angry husbands is not a good idea. I'll help you find and interrogate whichever ones you think had a reason to kill Andy, but we will not shoot them. You understand? We'll report whatever we find to the San Juan County Sheriff and hope for the best. Manny and the Santa Fe County Sheriff down here might be able to press them to actually do something."

"Why, I declare, Mr. Lopez, you are a true gentleman," Ruby said in her best imitation of a southern drawl. "That's downright gallant of you."

Fernando laughed.

"But I still might have to shoot one of the bastards!" Ruby said. "We'll see how it goes."

"You want me to come over and pick you up?" Fernando asked.

"Hell, no, we're not even dressed yet," Ruby said. "We'll meet you at your office, say eleven o'clock? Okay?"

Fernando agreed and spent the next couple of hours on his patio drinking too much coffee. He felt good and buzzed by the time he left to meet Ruby and Tessa. After locking his Smith & Wesson in the glove compartment of the Cherokee just in case he needed it, he drove around the Paseo and up Canyon Road to his office. Ready for anything the day would bring.

He found Ruby and Tessa sitting in Ruby's Honda waiting for him. They climbed out of the Honda as soon as he came to a stop. Looked like they'd had a hard night. Both of them wore jeans and T-shirts, hair looking like it hadn't been combed in days.

"Am I driving?" Fernando asked, surprised when they started to get into his Cherokee.

"You're driving," Ruby said, slamming her door shut. "We drank too much wine last night talking about funeral arrangements and all that good stuff. Then Blaine stopped by and we drank more wine."

"No problem," Fernando said, waiting for them to buckle up and then driving down Canyon Road and around the Paseo to Highway 285/84. As they passed by the Tesuque exit and the Santa Fe Opera, Ruby and Tessa started discussing where to hold and who to invite to a memorial for Andy. One of them would toss out a name and the other would say, "No, she's a bitch!" or "No, he's an asshole!" The only thing they'd agreed on by the time they cleared Española and entered the Chama River Valley was that they would hold the memorial in the outdoor patio of the Abiquiu Inn, which they both liked.

"So who will you invite?" Fernando asked. "Don't you like any of your neighbors?"

"Nope," Ruby said.

"Not much," Tessa added.

"Oh hell, the fucker doesn't deserve a memorial anyway," Ruby said. "Just invite the usual schmucks you hang out with."

"Anyone from Santa Fe?" Fernando asked.

"Just you and Blaine," Ruby said. "He gave me some bullets, after all."

Ruby patted her purse, which told Fernando that she'd brought along that old Glock pistol. What he feared. He stifled a curse and squeezed the steering wheel so tight his knuckles turned white.

Fernando drove past the Abiquiu Inn, where they saw several people seated on the outdoor patio eating lunch. Then he passed by the road leading to the town of Abiquiu on top of the mesa, where the famous Georgia O'Keeffe House looked over the highway below, the Chama River, and the distant mesas receding to the horizon in shades of pink, gray, and white. Finally he slowed down when he approached the collection of storefront shops and galleries along the highway and stopped in front of Tessa's tumbledown gallery.

Abiquiu Fine Art, as it was called, had seen better days. Or so it seemed to Fernando as he regarded the old adobe structure with cracked stucco and peeling blue windowsills. He noticed a frame extension had been added to the rear of the building, no doubt to serve as a residence for Tessa and Andy. The three of them climbed out of the Cherokee and walked to the front door. While Tessa fumbled with the key and then the security system, Ruby looked around the grounds and scowled. "I don't like this place," she said to Fernando, not bothering to explain herself. "I'm trying to get Tessa to move to Santa Fe where we can help each other out."

Once inside, Fernando saw a few small counters and locked glass cabinets displaying the usual Southwestern pottery and jewelry. A stack of small handmade rugs, Navajo or Mexican, draped over the end of one counter. On the walls hung paintings and other arts and crafts items for sale. Compared to the glitzy galleries on Santa Fe's Canyon Road, Abiquiu Fine Arts looked positively impoverished. He couldn't imagine many tourists stopping here or buying anything if they did. He could see why Ruby would want Tessa to join her in Santa Fe.

They walked on through the gallery into the residential section of the building where they stopped for a quick lunch. Tessa made them green chile and cheese sandwiches and glasses of iced tea. Fernando listened while Ruby and Tessa made plans for how to proceed. Tessa explained why she thought Bud Powers and Ray Sandoval were the two most likely to have shot Andy, because the entire community knew Andy had been fooling around with their wives.

"Okay, enough talk, Ruby said finally. "Let's start with Bud Powers. Where can we find him?"

"He works the day shift at the Abiquiu Inn, just down the street," Tessa said. "He should be at the front desk."

So after Tessa locked the gallery and reset the security system, the three of them climbed back into the Cherokee. Fernando drove back down the highway a few hundred feet to the Abiquiu Inn, a sprawling property that included the main building and outdoor patio-restaurant in front, with rustic casitas and two-suite duplexes scattered across the grounds. The buildings were all adobe or faux adobe decked out with porticos, vigas, gardens, and lots of other Southwestern touches that screamed New Mexico. Abiquiu, New Mexico.

Ruby and Tessa jumped out of the Cherokee first, leaving Fernando behind. That left him time to have second thoughts about what they were doing before he opened his door and joined them.

"Suck it up, Tessa," Ruby said. "Let's do this!"

Tessa stiffened and stomped up the wooden ramp leading to the front door of the inn. Ruby and Fernando followed.

Tessa burst through the front door and yelled, "Bud Powers!"

5

Tessa's bravado disappeared instantly when she saw the man behind the counter. She sighed and exhaled loudly, as Bud Powers turned to look at her, one arm in a shoulder sling and the other fumbling with a walker, trying to move the walker across the wooden floor. Hunched over and moving in spastic jerks, Powers looked as though he were in a great deal of pain. "Tessa?"

Tessa softened her tone. "What happened to you?"

"Oh, someone T-boned me in Española a couple of weeks ago," Bud said. "I got a ruptured disc that's not healing properly, so the docs think I need surgery. A metal rod inserted, maybe. I don't know yet."

"Jesus," Tessa said.

Ruby stepped forward, not about to let their purpose be diverted. "Were you down at Nageezi two days ago when Andy was shot?"

"No, why would I be in Nageezi," Bud said. Then he turned to Tessa. "I heard about Andy. I'm sure sorry for your loss, Tessa. Even though I didn't like him much, I wouldn't want any man to be shot down like that."

Tears formed in Tessa's eyes.

"He was a real ladies man, that's for sure," Bud said. "He fooled around with lotta women hereabouts, but I don't hold a grudge, especially not now. Wouldn't be the Christian thing to do."

"Where were you Saturday morning?" Ruby asked, not giving up.

"I was at Christus Saint Vincent Hospital in Santa Fe getting a CT-scan," Bud said. "Sally was with me. You can ask her."

Ruby frowned. "Well, then, do you know anyone else in Abiquiu who'd want to kill Andy?"

Bud clucked his tongue. "I reckon a number of men around here might want to punch Andy, but kill him? I find that hard to believe. That just doesn't happen in Abiquiu."

Fernando walked back outside and let them talk. Now that the tension seemed to be defused, he wasn't worried about anyone getting shot, at least not here at the Abiquiu Inn. Outside, he leaned against the Cherokee and surveyed the Abiquiu landscape. From where he stood he could see the adobe fence surrounding the Georgia O'Keeffe House up on top of the mesa. He remembered chasing Ruby's ex-husband Jimmy Mackey all over these parts. At one point Mackey hid out in Georgia O'Keeffe's fallout shelter. Fernando had no idea that O'Keeffe even had a fallout shelter back then. He still had a hard time believing it. Georgia O'Keeffe?

After the chit-chat ended inside, Ruby and Tessa walked out of the Abiquiu Inn and joined him. "I don't know, maybe he's faking it," Ruby said, still scowling.

Fernando laughed. "I don't think so, Ruby."

"Yeah, well, let's go pay a visit to Ray Sandoval then," Ruby said. At this point Ruby had taken charge. Tessa just went along quietly.

They climbed back into the Cherokee. Fernando sat in the driver's seat waiting for instructions. None came. "So where are we going?" he asked.

Tessa spoke finally, almost reluctantly. "Ray works at Ghost Ranch. He manages the stables."

Fernando pulled out on the highway and headed west past Abiquiu Lake toward Ghost Ranch, which he knew all too well. He'd spent way too much time there chasing Jimmy Mackey and later Cowboy Jack and his kid brother in that Taos vendetta business. The damn place was supposed to be haunted. He remembered the history as he negotiated the highway. Rumors began in the 1880s when the owners, the Archuleta Brothers, named the property *Rancho de los Brujos*. The brothers, notorious cattle rustlers, stole cattle and horses and hid them in the box canyon behind the ranch. They chose the name Ranch of the Witches to scare away farmers and ranchers who came looking for their stolen livestock. Rumor had it the brothers murdered those who continued to search for their animals and buried the bodies in the canyon or tossed them into wells. Ghost stories soon followed. Locals claimed to hear the voices of the murdered victims in the howling winds blowing through the canyon. The Archuleta Brothers also met a grisly fate. One brother killed the other during an argument over booty. The surviving brother died soon after, hung by an angry posse for a life of cattle rustling and murder. Both brothers joined the ghostly ranks, according to the legend.

When he saw the entrance, Fernando turned right on the primitive road leading into the sprawling property, surrounded by distant mesas and jagged cliffs. The road curved around toward the massive Kitchen Mesa, with a maze of roads connecting the various buildings off to the left.

He remembered the horse corrals were located on the back loop behind the Lower Pavilion. Most of the guest casitas and other accommodations were further down the main drive. So he made a quick left-hand turn and followed the signs to the stable office.

Ahead they saw workers on a flatbed truck unloading bales of hay at the first barn. A tall, thin man wearing a western hat stood off to the side holding a clipboard in his hands. He scribbled on a stack of papers as the workers unloaded the bales, maybe recording the number of bales. In addition to his hat, he wore jeans, a western shirt, and a leather vest.

"That's Ray," Tessa said. "Be careful, he has a bad temper."

Great, Fernando thought. If anything could set off a man's temper, it would be accusing him of murder. Still, he pulled over to the side of the road, resigned to see this day through.

Ruby jumped out of the Cherokee first. She swaggered up to Sandoval, followed by Tessa and Fernando, who held back. "We need to ask you some questions, Sandoval," Ruby said bluntly.

Sandoval turned to face Ruby, confused. "Who are you?"

Then Tessa stepped up and pushed Ruby back. "Ray, it's Tessa. Were you at Nageezi the day Andy was killed?"

Sandoval lowered his clipboard and stared at the two women. "No. Why would I? I don't give a damn about Chaco Canyon."

"Were you involved in the shooting?" Tessa asked.

"So that's why you're here," Sandoval snarled.

Now Ruby pushed Tessa back. "Answer the question," she said. "Did you kill Andy?"

Sandoval turned to address Tessa. "Let me tell you something about your piece of shit husband. He deserved to be shot after all the marriages he wrecked around here. He wasn't worth the bullet that killed him. I only wish I could have been the one to pull the trigger. There's no one around here who gives a tinker's damn that he's dead. Good riddance to the sonofabitch!"

Once gain tears formed in Tessa's eyes.

Tessa's tears infuriated Ruby. She charged halfway to Sandoval and shouted, "Hey, maybe the problem was you couldn't satisfy your wife! Ever think of that, you bastard!"

At that Sandoval tossed his clipboard and stepped into the barn. When he came out he had a pitchfork in his hand and moved toward Ruby with the pitchfork. "You fucking bitches don't know what you're talking about. Now get the hell out of here before I jab you!"

"Hah! The hell you will!" Ruby spit back at Sandoval, her right hand reaching into her purse.

Fernando realized Ruby was reaching for Jimmy's old Glock. He moved quickly to prevent a shooting and God knows what else. "Take it easy, Ruby," he said, grabbing her from behind and wrapping his arms around her waist so she couldn't withdraw the pistol. Then he lifted her off the ground, turned her around, and gave her a push toward the Cherokee.

"Get that bitch out of here," Sandoval said, still coming forward.

"We're leaving," Fernando said. "They've said their piece."

Sandoval still didn't back off. He began making jabbing motions toward Fernando with the pitchfork coming forward. The pitchfork came closer and closer to Fernando's face.

Finally Fernando had had enough. He waited until Sandoval lunged at him and then grabbed the shaft just below the tines, pushing them away from his face. Then he kicked Sandoval in the groin as hard as he could.

Sandoval yelped and dropped the handle of the pitchfork. Then he fell to his knees grimacing in pain.

Fernando turned and walked away, joining Ruby and Tessa at the Cherokee. The three of them climbed into the Jeep and took off, leaving Sandoval kneeling in the dust cursing at them.

"That went well," Fernando said, turning onto the highway.

Ruby gave him a dirty look. "Don't you dare say I told you so. Just get us back to Santa Fe."

"Yes, ma'am."

6

Fernando slept late next morning, after their fiasco in Abiquiu. They didn't get back to Santa Fe until nearly seven o'clock yesterday evening. Ruby insisted they stop at Tessa's gallery before hitting the road, so Tessa could pack enough clothes and toiletries to get her through a couple of weeks in Santa Fe. Tessa didn't seem terribly fond of the idea but followed her older sister's orders. In fact, Tessa didn't say much of anything. She seemed to have withdrawn into her shell of sadness over her cheating husband Andy's death.

Since it was late, he dressed first and then went into the kitchen for his coffee. Estelle had left an empty pot, so he brewed himself a cup of Sumatra in his Keurig and sat down to read the morning *Independent*. He skimmed quickly through the newspaper, finding nothing new about the shooting in Nageezi. So he tossed the *Independent* in the trash where it belonged. Then he brewed himself a second up of coffee and went outside to the patio. He loved to sit on their patio, surrounded by tall cottonwoods and Estelle's rose garden. For years it had been his private place, his refuge from the world outside the adobe wall that enclosed their property.

He and Estelle had purchased their 1920s adobe on Acequia Madre Street early in their marriage. They'd preserved the small adobe pretty much as it was when they bought it, except for minor modernizations. He took great pride in preserving this small piece of history on a street blighted by gentrification. Up and down Acequia Madre wealthy newcomers had bought and remodeled the houses into million-dollar mansions. The over-class, he called them, rich people who had turned Santa Fe into Disneyland Southwest. As a result long-time Santa Feans could no longer afford to live in Santa Fe. The median price of a house in Santa Fe County was approaching one million dollars. He didn't consider himself a class warrior, but clearly something had to be done. The economic disparities had become obscene.

He couldn't decide whether to head down to his office or to spend the morning working in the garden. Estelle had been bugging him for days to clear away the dead leaves and stalks now that Fall was fast approaching. Time to make room for Fall flowers, she'd said, planning to go to her favorite nursery this coming weekend. He knew he shouldn't keep putting it off, but....

The ringing of his cell phone on the patio bench made the decision for him. He saw the familiar name and clicked the accept icon.

"Fernando, I have some news finally," Antonio said. "We just received the ballistics report on the Dejon shooting in Nageezi. It wasn't Jack Lacy. He wasn't the shooter."

Fernando felt a sense of relief, although he wasn't surprised. "How so? How do you know?" He asked.

"Because Dejon was shot with an AR-15," Antonio said. "That's too messy, and it doesn't have enough range. I know for a fact that Lacy uses a SAKO TRG 42. The SAKO is one of the world's best sniper rifles, made in Finland. It has a range of eleven hundred meters, twice as long as the AR-15. And the SAKO uses a larger sixty-seven millimeter cartridge."

"Well, that makes sense," Fernando said. "I find it hard to believe that a professional assassin would come all the way to Santa Fe to shoot a nobody like Andy Dejon."

Fernando decided not to tell Antonio about Ruby and Tessa's crazy theory that Dejon's murderer was one of the cuckolded husbands whose wives Dejon had bedded. Nor their trip to Abiquiu yesterday to confront and possibly shoot whichever cuckold they decided to finger. Too preposterous to repeat. Not to mention embarrassing, given his involvement.

Antonio laughed. "Yeah, so now we're looking at some of the hotheads who blocked the road into Chaco. Looks like some of them are outside agitators for the big oil companies who've done this before, most notably at the Keystone Pipeline confrontations. These guys are like oil industry storm troopers, paid to disrupt and intimidate."

"I'm sure the agitators are in the pockets of the big oil companies in some way," Fernando replied.

"So listen, I'm thinking about paying Jack Lacy a friendly visit, just showing up at his hotel room," Antonio said. "What do you think? Would you come with me? I mean, Lacy and I were friends once, so why not?"

"Yeah, but you're a cop and he's...well, not exactly your typical law-abiding citizen."

"I know, that's why I thought it would be good if you came along," Antonio said. "Like friends, a friendly visit. And since you have that Steyr sniper rifle, the two of you could talk shop."

Fernando laughed. "Un-huh."

"I take that as a yes," Antonio said. "I got his room number. He has the corner room on the third floor overlooking the Plaza. Say we meet about eleven o'clock in the lobby? Afterwards you can treat me to lunch at the Shed."

"Okay, I guess," Fernando said, against his better judgment.

Antonio clicked off before Fernando could change his mind.

Not what he had planned to do today, but so it goes. Sometimes he thought his life had been all happenstance. We like to plan and think we're in control of our lives, but are we really?

Let that be the question of the day, Fernando decided.

Feeling a bit put upon by Antonio, Fernando went inside and cleaned up the kitchen before leaving. Estelle liked a clean kitchen, and a happy Estelle was easier to live with than an unhappy Estelle. He grabbed his holster on the way out of the house and locked the kitchen door. Outside he had second thoughts about the Smith & Wesson. Maybe it would be better to leave it in his Cherokee for now. Might not be a good idea to appear at the door of a professional assassin wearing a gun–it could give the man the wrong impression. So he locked the big gun in his glove compartment, out of sight.

Fernando drove down Acequia Madre to the Paseo and around to Alameda Street, where he liked to park. Making sure to lock the Cherokee, he ambled up Cathedral Place to La Fonda, his favorite hotel in Santa Fe. In fact, if Estelle ever kicked him out of the house, he figured he would head straight to La Fonda. The 100-year-old hotel had a history as long and turbulent as Santa Fe's itself. Local lore claimed it was as haunted as the Palace of the Governors. He knew the history well and everything that came with it, including ghosts.

Built on the southeast corner of the Santa Fe Plaza, La Fonda was preceded by a series of inns and hotels dating from the early 17th century. From its earliest days, long before the Santa Fe Trail opened up the city in 1821, criminals and misfits were executed by hanging either at the existing inn or on its property. The murder and mayhem continued after New Mexico became a U.S. Territory in 1848, when the inn became the U.S. Hotel. The most infamous murder occurred in 1867, when a member of the Territorial Legislature gunned down John P. Slough, Chief Justice of the Territorial Supreme Court. But Chief Justice Slough did not go quietly. In fact, Slough's ghost continued to haunt the hotel as it became the Exchange Hotel and then was replaced in 1922 by the current La Fonda, which happened to operate as a Harvey House from 1926 to 1968.

Over time Slough's ghost joined a gallery of other ghosts and apparitions walking the hotel's hallways. Fernando didn't recall all of them. He did remember a salesman who gambled away his company's money and then proceeded to throw himself in a well where La Plazuela is now located. The ghost of the salesman is said to appear from time to time in La Plazuela. Then there was the ghost of a man wearing a black coat who wanders the upstairs hallways looking for something, who knows what. And the ghost of a young woman murdered on her wedding night. And others, most of them nameless and forlorn as history itself.

Or so the legend of haunted La Fonda went, for what it was worth. Fernando neither believed nor disbelieved in ghosts, but he knew he'd seen some sort of apparition at Chaco Canyon and again at Painted Skull Ranch in Taos, call it what you will. And the more he thought about it, it made perfect sense that as places age and acquire a history, they would also acquire ghosts. Ghosts come with history, just as places and landscapes have memory. Something like that.

Still thinking about ghosts, Fernando entered La Fonda and walked down the gilded hallway into the lobby, a treasure house of Southwestern art and furniture. From the tiled floors, the heavy wooden ceiling beams, and the Native American décor, the room screamed Old Santa Fe. He'd been coming here for fifty odd years and he still found it exciting. The place had a certain magic, he couldn't explain it any better than that. Ghosts notwithstanding.

"Fernando!" Antonio called from over by the stairway.

Fernando waved and made his way through the late summer crowd of tourists. There was already a long line of people waiting to be seated at La Plazuela for an early lunch.

"You sure about this?" Fernando asked, joining Antonio. He noticed that Antonio was not armed either.

Antonio shrugged. "No, not really."

"I mean, why do you want to do this? What's the point?"

"To find out why he's here," Antonio said. "And I don't know...we used to be friends, like I said. We were close."

Fernando nodded. "Whatever you say."

They walked up two flights of steps to the third floor.

"He has the first room here on the corner," Antonio said. "Let me do the talking, okay? I only hope he recognizes me."

"Be my guest," Fernando said, motioning for Antonio to go ahead. He stood back while Antonio walked up to the door.

The big man knocked lightly with his knuckles and then waited. When there was no response, he knocked again.

"Come in–" came a voice from inside the room, a flat, dry, inflectionless voice.

Antonio opened the door and stepped inside. Fernando followed.

"Freeze!" ordered the same flat, dry voice.

Fernando glanced to his left, where he saw a tall, thin man dressed in black holding a snub-nose pistol pointed directly at them.

7

Fernando and Antonio froze.

"Who are you? What do you–" the man in black barked. Then a faint smile rippled the corners of his mouth. "Tony? Is that you?"

Antonio saluted.

"Well, I'll be damned," Lacy said. He lowered his pistol and walked over to Antonio. "Damn, you're even bigger than I remember."

"Hah! I think I still might be growing," Antonio said.

Lacy laughed. "I heard about your divorce and that you'd moved down to New Mexico. Our old friend Sam Lawrence said he thought you were working as a cop and living in a cabin somewhere. Is that right?"

Fernando noticed Lacy talked with his mouth nearly closed in something of a grimace. His lips barely moved, his voice seeming to come from somewhere deep in his body.

Antonio nodded. "Pretty much. I've been living in a cabin I built out in the Pecos Wilderness and working for the Santa Fe Police Department. Seemed like a good way to keep busy doing pretty much what I was doing in Iraq. Helped me get through my Post Traumatic Stress Disorder. I feel much calmer now. I'm ready to take it easy, so I turned in my resignation effective immediately. I'm no longer a cop."

"Wait, are you serious?" Fernando asked, taken by surprise. This was news to him. He wanted to know more but realized this wasn't the time to grill Antonio. That would have to wait.

"Jack, this is my good friend Fernando," Antonio said. "He wanted to come along and meet you."

"Pleased to me you," Lacy said.

"Likewise," Fernando responded.

Lacy checked his watch. "Well, it's almost lunchtime, why don't we go down to the bar and talk."

"You read my mind," Antonio said.

Lacy put away his snub-nose in a concealed carry holster on his belt.

He ushered them out of the room and made sure the door locked securely behind them. They walked down the stairway to the lobby. The bar, one of Fernando's favorites, branched off the south side of the lobby.

Fernando let the two old friends go first. He followed along behind, noticing how stiffly Lacy walked. He didn't appear to be in the best of health, which struck Fernando as odd for a professional assassin.

They took a private, corner table away from the tourists.

Pam, one of the newer servers at the La Fonda Bar, smiled at Fernando and came over to take their orders. With short, kinky red hair and tattoos up and down her arms and around her neck, Pam brought a splash of color wherever she went. "What can I get you gentlemen?" she asked.

Antonio smiled and glanced around the table. He liked to joke with Pam. "I don't see any gentlemen here, but you can get me a Coors draft."

"Speak for yourself," Fernando said to Antonio. "I'll have my usual, a Modelo draft."

Lacy ordered last. "Bring me two fingers of your best Scotch and a cup of coffee, please."

"Will do."

The three of them watched Pam walk back to the bar.

"I wonder where else she has tattoos," Antonio said.

Fernando laughed. "Don't even go there."

Lacy said nothing until Pam returned with their drinks. Then he took a drink of Scotch and turned to Antonio. "So why did you really come to see me? I know you're aware of what I do for a living."

Antonio choked on his Coors for a moment, coughing.

With that, Lacy turned to Fernando and said, "My guess is that you know all about me too. What you might have read or heard is true. I eliminate corrupt politicians and businessmen. For that I'm paid large sums of money. Most of my work has been in the Mideast and Europe, on occasion Southeast Asia. I haven't been back to the states for many years."

Fernando didn't know how to respond, so he turned to Antonio.

"So why did you come back now?" Antonio asked, still coughing. "I guess that's why I wanted to come see you. I was curious."

"A job?" Fernando asked.

Lacy sighed. "Partly a job, but the job had to be called off. Now the employer wants a refund of the advance. I don't give refunds."

"Who's the employer?" Fernando asked.

Lacy stared at Fernando with cold, steel gray eyes. "Let's don't talk business now. Just relax and enjoy the moment."

Antonio agreed with Lacy. "Yeah, let's forget business. So what's the other reason you're here? A vacation maybe? Some rest and relaxation? Santa Fe has a lot to offer."

Lacy smiled. "So I'm told. This is my first time here. If I like it, I might decide to stay. Why not, it has a long history of accepting controversial figures with, shall we say, blemished reputations seeking anonymity. High profile people like John Ehrlichman, Joseph Epstein, and most recently John Eastman. Santa Fe seems like the ideal place to become anonymous."

"So you're quitting? You're hanging it up after all these years?" Antonio asked, hopefully.

Lacy looked uncomfortable. He pushed his coffee away and twirled the Scotch glass in his hand. Finally he looked up at Antonio. "No choice, you see. I think the war has finally caught up with me. I know you're familiar with Post Traumatic Stress Disorder, but there are other conditions that affect just as many of us: Gulf War Syndrome, and in my case Burn Pit Exposure."

Antonio nodded.

Lacy took a long drink of Scotch and then said, "What I'm trying to say is that I was diagnosed with Glioblastoma a few months ago. Brain cancer."

"Shit!" Antonio said.

"How long do you have?" Fernando asked, realizing too late how callous his question sounded. He had an aunt who developed Glioblastoma and was dead within the year.

Lacy shrugged. "A year, maybe eighteen months."

"Aren't there any treatments?" Antonio asked.

"What's the point?" Lacy asked. "We all have a one-way ticket to the same terminal. The final deployment."

Instantly silence descended on the table like a giant curtain, cutting off dialogue, isolating each of them in their own space, with their own thoughts. They finished their drinks, none of them wanting another. When Pam brought their check, Lacy took a one-hundred dollar bill out of his wallet and tossed it on the table. He pushed his chair back from the table and crossed his legs.

Lacy smiled. "Tony, you probably don't remember this. I don't know, maybe you do. Remember the time that crazy Sam Lawrence threw a grenade at a bunker and it slipped out of his hand and landed in front of him?"

Antonio laughed. "I do! Absolutely! I've never seen anyone hit the dirt faster than old Sam. He was lucky he didn't blow his head off, crazy fucker."

After that the mood at the table lightened. Antonio and Lacy began swapping war stories. Fernando saw his opportunity to get away, so he excused himself and hightailed it out of La Fonda.

Outside the fresh air and sunshine never felt so inviting. Just to be alive, that was all that mattered. At the moment he needed to get away from whatever it was he'd just witnessed. He didn't know how to read Lacy, and he didn't know what to make of Antonio's sudden announcement that he'd turned in his badge. Why now? Was it really because of Lacy's visit?

Had Antonio been planning to join Lacy, before the news of Lacy's cancer ended that fantasy?

Fernando walked to his Cherokee and drove back around the Paseo to Canyon Road and up to his office. He noticed Ruby's Honda Accord parked by her gallery as he pulled into their parking lot. Ruby hadn't said a word to him on their way back from Abiquiu yesterday, clearly pissed at him. As if it were his fault their day had gone awry and the chances of finding a cuckolded husband who'd shot and killed Andy was slim to none.

Fernando turned off the ignition and set the brake on the Cherokee, lingering a few moments to brood about his encounter with Jack Lacy. He had as many questions now as he had before their meeting. If Lacy was in Santa Fe to do a job, then who was the target? And why was the hit cancelled? Not to mention Antonio's announcement that he'd turned in his resignation. Why retire now if not to join Lacy? Antonio was a good fifteen years away from retirement age. Didn't figure.

Finally he gave up. Nothing seemed to make sense anymore. He climbed out of the Cherokee and headed for Ruby's gallery, which she'd named Three Cities of Spain after a historic Canyon Road restaurant that closed decades ago. He opened the front door and stepped inside. The gallery's walls and shelves were a riot of color: vibrant acrylic and oil paintings hung on the walls, while colorful ceramics filled the shelves that Ruby added to accommodate the pottery produced in her pottery co-op down in the Railyard District.

Not seeing anyone, Fernando called, "Ruby?"

"Yeah, we're back here," Ruby said, sticking her head around the corner of the little room she called the coffee room or sometimes the lunch room.

Fernando found the two sisters sitting at the wooden counter Ruby had installed after inheriting the building. She'd added a refrigerator and microwave and cabinets over the counter.

"Glad to see you're in a better mood," Fernando said. "I was worried you'd still be mad at me."

Ruby laughed. "Nah, I wasn't really mad at you, just pissed the day had turned out so badly. A waste of time. I don't know what I was thinking."

"You were just trying to help," Fernando said.

"Turned out to be a wild goose chase," Ruby added. "Bud Powers and Ray Sandoval were the two most likely suspects. The rest of the bastards are too worthless to shoot."

Tessa smiled. "Anyway, I found Andy's life insurance policy. That eases the pain, if you know what I mean," she said, winking.

"Pull up a chair from the office and join us for lunch," Ruby said. "We picked up some tacos at La Choza on the way into town. There's beer in the fridge."

Fernando laughed. "Thanks, but I just came from the La Fonda Bar. I'm on my way home now. I just wanted to make sure you were okay."

"Yeah, we're okay," Ruby said. "We didn't shoot anybody, if that's what you mean."

"Did you talk to the San Juan County Sheriff's Office? Anything new in their investigation?"

Ruby shook her head. "That's a laugh. A deputy named Mike Rodriguez came by and asked a few questions. He said there were over a hundred people present at the shooting and that they have no leads, nothing."

Fernando wasn't surprised but didn't say anything.

"Here's the card he gave me," Ruby said, handing the card to Fernando. "Do me a favor, call Rodriguez and see if you can get anything more out of him. Maybe he'll talk to you since you were a big-shot Santa Fe Police detective. They must be doing something, yes?"

Fernando took the card and put it in his shirt pocket. Big shot? That was news to him.

Tessa smiled as he walked out of the gallery. No doubt about it, Andy Dejon must have had one handsome life insurance policy.

8

Back home, Fernando sat at the kitchen table eating a late lunch, a bowl of posole, the only leftovers he could find in the fridge. Lately he'd been too lazy to cook anything for lunch. He preferred leftovers, hot or cold it didn't matter. If no leftovers, then a quick turkey breast or cheese and green chile sandwich. Earlier today at La Fonda he'd broken his routine and had a Modelo before lunch, something he never did. He was a man of routines, a bit OCD according to Estelle and his daughters, both of whom considered him an old crank too rigid to change his ways. But so what? He'd earned his right to be an old crank.

When he finished the posole, he brewed himself a cup of coffee and took it outside to his favorite bench on the patio. He'd left a message at the San Juan County Sheriff's Office asking Deputy Mike Rodriguez to call him back. In the meantime he decided to take another look at the garden, just to size up how much work would be involved in clearing the brush, as Estelle wanted him to do. Looked like too much work for today, he decided, as he did pretty much every day. Better to put it off until tomorrow morning when he would be fresh and in a better mood. At the moment he was still flummoxed by Antonio's resignation announcement and Lacy's mysterious presence in Santa Fe.

The ringing of his cell phone on the bench interrupted his thoughts. He clicked accept.

"Mr. Lopez, this is Mike Rodriguez from the San Juan County Sherriff's Office returning your call," a friendly voice said. "How can I help you?"

"Thanks for calling back," Fernando said. "I'm a former Santa Fe Police detective now a private investigator. One of my clients is the wife of Andy Dejon, the man who was shot and killed at Nageezi. I'm wondering if there's been any breakthroughs in the case, anything new."

Rodriguez sighed. "Not really. We don't have many leads at this point. As best we can tell there were over a hundred people and dozens of cars at the murder scene. From the trajectory of the bullets we know the shooter fired from the road above the parking lot. Could have been a drive-by shooting, we don't know. No one we've interviewed so far claims to have seen the shooter. What we really need is video. We've put out several calls for information, especially video, but so far no one has come forward."

"I see," Fernando responded. "Do you know if anyone else there was seriously injured?"

"Not to our knowledge," Rodriguez said.

"Do you think it was a random shooting, or do you think Dejon could have been targeted?"

"Well, only two bullets were fired and both hit the victim in the middle of the back," Rodriguez said. "Sure seems like a targeted killing."

"Yeah...seems like it, I guess," Fernando said.

"Although, it's hard to figure out why someone like Dejon would be targeted," Rodriguez added. "Someone who owns a small gallery in Abiquiu and volunteers for a nonprofit? Doesn't really make sense. Unless someone had a personal grudge against Dejon."

"Okay, thanks," Fernando said and clicked off.

Given the short staffing of county sheriffs offices across New Mexico, and the simple logistics of the crime scene at Nageezi, Fernando doubted Andy Dejon's killer would ever be found. Unless, that is, Jack Lacy knew something about the killing and would be more forthcoming.

After a while, sitting idle on the patio, Fernando began to feel guilty. He had plenty of time to clear the dead brush from their garden. Why put off till tomorrow what he could do today? Resigned, he walked to the garage and retrieved his gardening gloves and a small shrub rake. Then he went to work, raking the dead flowers, stalks, and leaves into one big pile, which he then carried to a mulch bed near their adobe wall. Finished, he replaced his gloves and rake in the garage and was about to head to the shower when he saw a Jeep turn into his driveway. Antonio's Jeep Wrangler.

Antonio pulled up behind Fernando's Cherokee. Then the big man climbed slowly, haltingly out of his Wrangler.

"What's going on?" Fernando asked. "Why did you resign?"

Antonio ignored the question. "Can we talk?"

Fernando threw open his arms and said, "Why not." He walked back to the patio, Antonio following.

Fernando took his usual seat on the bench, while Antonio sat in a facing Adirondack chair, his long legs stretching out over half the patio. He looked uncomfortable with what he had to say.

"Here's the deal," Antonio began. "Jack and I go back a long way. He saved my life once on a convoy in Iraq. I owe him big time. I didn't want my job as a cop to get in the way of our friendship. I knew we would talk about what he does for a living, which would present a problem since I was a cop. You understand what I'm saying? I could never turn him in, even if my job required it. So I resigned to save us all an awkward situation."

Fernando shook his head, not sure of how to respond.

"Anyway, the Chief will take me back in a second, once Jack leaves Santa Fe, Antonio added."

"What if Lacy doesn't leave Santa Fe?" Fernando asked. "He said he might stay here and go underground."

Antonio shrugged. "I can't imagine him staying here. He likes a big city where he can be anonymous, truly anonymous. We'll see what happens."

Fernando nodded. "So what did Lacy say? What did you learn from him that you don't want to report to law enforcement?"

"I'll tell you, but it has to be off the record," Antonio said. "You understand? Just between you and me. It goes no further."

"Understood," Fernando said.

"First, the hit that had to be called off was on Dee Highland."

Fernando erupted. "Dee Highland? The Interior Secretary of the United States! Jesus Christ, Antonio!"

Antonio raised his hand. "Fortunately for Highland, the event was cancelled because of the protest. She spoke instead at the Bureau of Indian Affairs Office in Albuquerque. She didn't go near the protesters at Chaco Canyon."

Fernando shook his head in disbelief. "Did Lacy identify his client? The group that was paying him to kill Highland?"

"No, but when you think about it, it's not hard to figure out who would order the hit," Antonio said.

"Some group connected to the fossil fuel industry, I suppose," Fernando responded.

Antonio nodded. "But here's the rest of the story. Now the client wants their advance back, two hundred fifty thousand dollars. Jack refuses to give it back, so the client has enlisted another local hit man to get it back one way or another, whatever it takes."

Fernando frowned. "Local hit man? In Santa Fe?"

"That's what Jack said."

"An assassin to assassinate an assassin," Fernando said, mostly to himself. "I suppose it makes sense, but I didn't know Santa Fe was that well-stocked with assassins?"

Antonio laughed.

"So does Lacy have any idea who this other local hit man might be?" Fernando asked.

Antonio shook his head. "He wouldn't say. He said he didn't want to get me involved, that he would take care of it himself."

"Maybe so, but he doesn't look like he's in the best of health," Fernando replied. "You saw him."

Antonio lowered his head. "Yeah."

The two of them sat on the patio in silence for several minutes, each of them lost in his own thoughts. By this time the sun had begun setting behind the cottonwoods on Acequia Madre. The leaves of the cottonwoods were already tinged with yellow. The late summer, early fall weather now carried a chill. Soon Fiesta would be here and then winter. At 7,000 feet above sea level Santa Fe could get damn cold in the winter, something Fernando wasn't looking forward to. He hated the cold with a passion. Especially this year, now that he had decided to retire and Antonio had just submitted his resignation. Seemed like everything was coming to an end.

The season of long shadows cast a melancholy shadow over them. Only the arrival of Estelle brought them out of their somber moods. Her Camry turned into the drive and parked beside Antonio's Wrangler. She jumped out of the car as spritely as ever, a trim woman with short gray hair and a winning smile. She wore a navy blue sweater and white pants as she walked over to the patio. "You two look positively morose," Estelle said. "Who died?"

Fernando smiled. Estelle had always managed to cheer him, even in his darkest moods. She'd been his lifeline for over forty years. He couldn't imagine his life without her.

"Just talking about retirement...things ending," Fernando said.

"Things ending means something else beginning," Estelle quipped and flashed them a big smile. "Are you staying for dinner, Antonio?"

"Nah, I've got to get back to Pecos. I'm not crazy about driving out there after dark anymore," Antonio said.

"Well, don't be a stranger," Estelle replied and walked into the house.

Antonio stood up to go.

"Keep me informed, okay?" Fernando said. "If there's anything I can do to help, let me know."

Antonio saluted.

"And be careful," Fernando said as Antonio walked away.

9

Fernando snapped awake when he heard his cell phone ring on the bedstand. He reached for his phone, glancing at the clock. Nine o'clock. He'd overslept again.

"Silva Archivada," Antonio said at the other end.

"What about him?" Fernando asked, wondering why Antonio was calling about Archivada, the head of the Sinaloa Cartel in New Mexico, an extremely dangerous man. They'd already had one battle with Archivada and his armed thugs on Upper Canyon Road, the shoot-out where the Mexican painter Ricardo Aragon was murdered and where Manny was wounded. They managed to save Ricardo's wife Maria, but Manny lost a kidney and part of his colon. Since then a sort of truce had developed between the cartel and the Santa Fe Police. Don't ask, don't tell, just look the other way had become the policy. Meanwhile, Archivada had bought the abandoned Forest Service building on Upper Canyon Road and the old Line Camp honky-tonk out in Pojoaque, where he claimed to be running a legitimate business.

"He's the hit man, the heavy who Jack's former client has hired to get the advance back from Jack," Antonio said.

"Wait a minute. I'm confused. How do you know this?" Fernando asked, barely awake.

Antonio sighed. "Jack told me this morning. Archivada called him last night. He wants a full reimbursement of the advance or there will be 'consequences,' as Archivada put it."

"Consequences," Fernando repeated.

"Yeah, and Jack refuses to return the money," Antonio said. "I think he's taking Archivada too lightly, he's a stubborn sonofabitch. Now he wants the two of us to accompany him as backup when he goes to meet Archivada this afternoon at the old Line Camp in Pojoaque. I don't know what Archivada's calling the place now, but I can guess what he's selling there."

"He's calling it Heaven's Door," Fernando said. "I drove by last week on my way to Chimayo."

"After the Bob Dylan song? 'Knocking on Heaven's Door'?"

"I guess," Fernando said, "except in his case the theme would be drugs, not religion."

Antonio laughed. "So what do you think? Are you in?"

Fernando paused, not really wanting to get involved in protecting a professional assassin from a Sinaloa Cartel chief. Talk about far-fetched, if not downright absurd. And yet he was curious, he had to admit.

"Okay then, I'll take that as a yes," Antonio said. "Why don't you pick us up in front of La Fonda at two p.m.," Antonio said. "We can all fit comfortably in your Cherokee."

So it was set, whether Fernando liked it or not. He would be protecting an assassin from the Sinaloa Cartel. Go figure.

Estelle had already left for work, so he made himself coffee and eggs for breakfast, showered, and then made himself a second cup of coffee before heading down to his office. Today he was determined to start packing. If he was going to retire, he had to start clearing out his office.

While he sipped his coffee, he reminisced about Line Camp, a Wild West honky-tonk out in Pojoaque. The infamous saloon/dancehall had been closed for years, but at one time Line Camp was one of the area's hot spots. It attracted a combustible crowd of rednecks and cowboys, hippies and revolutionaries that often as not erupted in brawls or even gunfire in the parking lot. He especially remembered radical lawyer Raoul Garcia hanging out at Line Camp. In fact, back then Raoul would sometimes hold office hours there, bringing with him a dangerous clientele of down-and-out hippies, fire-bombing revolutionaries, and outright criminals. Over the years Raoul's class warfare had taken a different tact. These days he imploded the obscenely wealthy from the inside, by taking their money through exorbitant charges. He could get away with it because he was hands-down the best criminal lawyer in the state of New Mexico.

Fernando had fond memories of Line Camp. When he was single, before he married Estelle and settled down, he'd been something of a regular at Line Camp. Those were his badass years. Looking back to those years made him happy. He didn't regret one damn thing of his youthful hijinks. Not one.

After finishing his coffee, he again got sidetracked reading the *Independent*, another long story about the shooting at Nageezi. Still no leads, according to the article. No one had come forward with new information or video that would help the investigation. Beginning to look like one of those cases that would never get solved. Someone had shot and killed Andy Dejon, but the San Juan County Sheriff's Office had absolutely no idea who or why and, given their track record, most likely would never know.

Fernando finally made it down to his office about Noon. Determined to start packing, he retrieved a couple of cardboard boxes from his closet and began emptying out his file cabinet. More stuff than he remembered, some of it crap he should have tossed out weeks ago. Old receipts, notes, photos, copies of invoices and other such material he'd collected since hanging up his shingle as a private investigator. He ended up saving most of the material, telling himself he might need the stuff for income tax purposes, even though most of it was years old. He filled the two cardboard boxes before stopping to take a break and quickly losing interest in the whole damn project. He sat back in his chair and looked over the mess he'd created, with two overflowing boxes of papers that he didn't know what to do with. Finally he carried the boxes back to the closet and left it at that. He'd done enough moving for today.

About Noon he went over to El Farol for lunch and chatted with the old regulars gathered in the bar. Then he stopped by Ruby's gallery and visited with her over a leisurely cup of coffee. Finally he made it back to his office, closed up for the day, and walked to his Cherokee. He checked the glove compartment to make sure his Smith & Wesson was there. It was, so he put on the holster and buckled up.

Fernando drove down to the Paseo and around to East Alameda Street. He took the first right on Cathedral Place and then turned left on San Francisco Street, across from La Fonda. Antonio and Jack Lacy were waiting out front of La Fonda for him. He was relieved to see that both of them wore open carry holsters. In addition, Lacy carried a gun bag, presumably for his fancy sniper rifle. You didn't walk into the den of the monster without being armed.

Antonio waved as Fernando pulled up. The big man jaywalked across the street and jumped into the front passenger seat. Jack Lacy climbed in the rear of the Cherokee.

"You ready for this?" Antonio asked.

Fernando laughed. "Sure. Can't wait!"

"Thanks for helping," Lacy said, tight-lipped and grimacing. "Tony told me you were a good friend."

Unable to hold his tongue, Fernando let the engine idle and said,

"You know, what really puzzles me is that the two of you were in the same unit in Iraq and have remained the best of friends. But Antonio, you went into law enforcement–and Jack, you went in the other direction, whatever you want to call it. I can't seem to wrap my mind around that disjunction. So what gives?"

Lacy shrugged. "I just continued doing what I was trained to do and had done in Iraq for years."

"It's true," Antonio added, coming to Lacy's defense. "I went into law enforcement for the same reasons. And if you think about it, there's not that much difference in what we do. Jack's also an enforcer, just like I am. He eliminates bad people."

"Yeah, that's fine, but who determines who's bad and needs to be eliminated?" Fernando asked.

Neither Antonio nor Lacy responded.

"Whatever," Fernando said, shaking his head. He didn't want to get in a philosophical debate about 'bad' people and who, if anyone, has the right to eliminate them.

Fernando shifted into gear and drove to the Paseo and then around to the entrance to Highway 84/285 West. The highway took him out of town past the Santa Fe Opera and the turnoff to the village of Tesuque. A few miles later he came to Buffalo Thunder, the huge casino resort owned by the Pojoaque Pueblo. Just beyond Buffalo Thunder the highway split, Highway 502 heading west toward Los Alamos, and Highway 84/285 shooting north toward Española and Taos. Line Camp was on the left side of 84/285 as it rounded the turn heading north.

Fernando looked for a parking lot or a fast food joint where he could pull over so Antonio and Lacy could stake out Line Camp, now Heaven's Door. Before their arrival, he wanted to show them the lay of the land. He'd done this once before, after he found out the Sinaloa Cartel had bought the old Line Camp building. When he saw a familiar gas station situated at the bottom of a small rise, he pulled into the station and drove behind the building. No one was around to bother them, so he took his binoculars out of the glove compartment and led them up the hill, through a patch of tumbleweed and snake grass.

The rise was just high enough for them to see over the commercial claptrap along the highway. They had a clear view of Heaven's Door, its new front windows covered with bright blue awnings. The building, though spruced up, seemed to sag in the middle as though tired from too many years of dancing and honky-tonking. Fernando saw two vehicles parked out front, a black Range Rover that he remembered from his first encounter with Silva Archivada and a black Toyota Sequoia.

"Looks pretty damn deserted for a bar and dancehall, if that's what it's supposed to be," Antonio said.

"I don't think there's any doubt about what he's selling there, and it's not music and dancing." Fernando replied.

Lacy, silent, studied the layout of the building, built alongside an arroyo that drained into the Rio Chupadero. He cleared his throat. "Two ways we could do this. The two of you could go down to the building and lure them outside somehow. Better yet, one of you could go down to the front door and the other one could come up from behind the building in that arroyo to make sure they don't run out the back door. Either way, I can take care of them from here."

With that, Lacy took an extra clip out of his jacket pocket and put it in his pants pocket.

Antonio glanced at Fernando and then back to Lacy. "Okay, but don't you want to talk first? Tell Archivada you're not going to give back the advance? Why make an enemy of the cartel unless you have to?"

"They don't bother me," Lacy said. "But sure, if you want to talk, let's pull up in front and talk. If they start shooting, I'll kill them right there. I'll kill all of them and be done with it."

Fernando held his tongue. He wondered just how the man could be so damn sure of himself. Especially in this situation.

Antonio just stared at Lacy, speechless.

10

"Okay, let's roll," Lacy said.

The three of them walked back down the hill to the Cherokee. They didn't bother with seatbelts. Fernando revved the big motor and squealed out onto the highway and around the corner on Highway 84/285.

Heaven's Door came into view immediately. Fernando made a sharp left turn into the parking lot in front of the building, across the lot from the Range Rover and Sequoia. He switched off the engine and set the brake and then turned to Antonio and Lacy. "It's your play."

Antonio nodded and opened his door. Lacy followed after placing his gun case flat on the floor beside the rear seat. Then Lacy took the lead, walking calmly to the front door. He didn't bother to knock. He walked right into the dance hall of the long building. When he did, a bell rang loudly to announce the visitors. The dance hall was empty, with a polished wooden floor and a stage for the band along one wall. To the left a door opened and two big gorillas walked out to greet them. Beefy but not as big or as muscular as Antonio, the two Sinaloa gunmen wore tight black sports uniforms and carried large pistols strapped to their waists. They could have been identical twins: round faces, stocky bodies, and short slicked back hair. They didn't exactly look like a happy welcoming committee.

"Where's Archivada?" Lacy said, disdainfully. He flashed them a look of contempt.

The smaller of the two thugs motioned toward the door.

Lacy brushed past the two of them and walked into what turned out to be a small office. Archivada sat behind a metal desk, his unbuttoned black shirt revealing a gold chain around his neck. His long black hair, tinged with gray, was slicked back with gel. The smile on his dark face faded when he saw Lacy walk in without hesitation and stand in the center of the room glaring at him, not about to take a seat. He fidgeted at his seat for a moment to get his composure back.

Then Lacy nodded to his two gorillas, who exited the building quickly. Moments later they heard a vehicle drive away out front of the building.

Not sure what was happening, Fernando remained standing but moved to one side of the room. Antonio remained behind Lacy.

"Mr. Lacy...I am aware of your reputation," Archivada said carefully. "I expected you to come alone."

"I brought two friends," Lacy said, smiling. "I think you know who they are."

Archivada said nothing.

"You wanted to talk," Lacy said, a statement.

Archivada nodded. "We have a problem, you see. Your recent employer paid you an advance to do a certain job that was never done, for whatever reason. Now they want their advance back. As simple as that."

Lacy shook his head. "I don't return advances. The cancellation was out of my control. As simple as that," he said, parroting Silva.

A sad expression came across Archivada's face. "This, you see, is not acceptable to your recent employer," Archivada said. "If you do not return the advance, there will be consequences. I am sorry to say this, but such is the truth."

Lacy frowned. "If there are consequences, there will be more consequences," he said back to Silva, a challenge.

"It pains me to hear this, Mr. Lacy. I thought you were both a reasonable and an honorable man."

"Hah!" Lacy laughed at Archivada. "There is no honor among men like you and me, Archivada. None!"

Archivada turned to Fernando. "Mr. Lopez, can you not talk to your friend? Once upon a time we negotiated a truce. Can't we do so again?"

Fernando shook his head. "Not my call, Archivada. That's between you and Lacy. As far as I'm concerned, our truce is still in effect. This is not my concern."

Archivada turned to Lacy. "You see, we can come to an agreement."

"I don't return advances," Lacy said, spitting the words at Archivada.

Archivada stared at Lacy. The tension in the room rose to the exploding point. Fernando moved further away from Archivada, as did Antonio.

One false move and the room would erupt in gunfire. An inferno.

"Here," Lacy said, taking a blue-and-gray cloth out of his back pocket. "It's a Dallas Cowboys crying towel I picked up at the Albuquerque airport. Give it to your employer."

Lacy threw the towel in Archivada's face and turned toward the door. Then he stopped abruptly and turned around to face Archivada. "You know where to find me... and I know where to find you."

Fernando waited until Lacy and Antonio walked out of the room. Then he waved to Archivada and followed them out to the Cherokee. Both men had their guns drawn, waiting for Fernando.

Without a word, Fernando climbed into the driver's seat and fired up the engine. He glanced back at the door to Heaven's Door and then backed up quickly and squealed out of the parking lot, bounding over the lip of a curve and onto Highway 84/285 heading east.

No one spoke until they cleared the Pojoaque commercial strip. "What do you think?" Fernando asked, looking at Lacy in the rear view mirror.

Lacy sighed. "Oh, he's not done with us. I probably should have killed him right there. I just wanted to see if he has any guts. He knows who he's dealing with. We'll see."

"I think he had a gun in his lap," Fernando said.

"He did, but he would have been dead before he got it out over the desk," Lacy replied. "He knew that, which is why he didn't try."

"So what now?" Antonio asked.

"We wait. It's his move," Lacy said.

"So you're not leaving town?" Fernando asked, unable to hide his disappointment.

Lacy turned away from the rear window where he had been watching to see if they were going to be followed. "I might stay a while. Like I said, Santa Fe's a good place to be anonymous. Get some R and R."

Fernando cleared the last hill and drove into Santa Fe. He left the highway at North Guadalupe Street and drove down to West San Francisco Street and up to La Fonda.

"Thanks," Antonio said as he climbed out of the Cherokee.

Lacy saluted as he jumped out of the Cherokee and then reached back in for his gun case.

Fernando breathed a sigh of relief as he drove off. Too much pressure, too much stress. Exactly the reason he'd left the Santa Fe Police Department. He decided to go back to his office and finish packing. Then maybe walk down to El Farol for Happy Hour. Ruby and the others would likely be there.

He drove to the end of San Francisco Street and over to East Alameda Street. At the Paseo he turned right and then made a quick left on Canyon Road. He already felt more relaxed now that he was in his own element.

That feeling lasted all of two minutes. As soon as he turned into his parking lot he saw the damage to his sign. Someone had taken an axe or some other heavy instrument and smashed his Private Eye sign in half. The left half of the wooden sign dangled crookedly from its post, while the right half lay flat in the dust. The sight of Ruby standing in the open door of his office, hands on her hips, told him there was more damage inside.

Cursing, Fernando pulled up beside Ruby's Accord and jumped out of the Cherokee. He walked over to his sign and surveyed the damage. It looked like a total loss, unless he could somehow bind the two halves together and refasten it to the posts. That might do at least until he could have another sign made. Then he remembered he was retiring so why should he give a damn? Let it lie there in the dust, a reminder of just why he was retiring.

He headed down the gravel path to his office. Ruby motioned for him to enter and stepped aside, a disgusted expression on her face. Looked like someone had jimmied the door with a crowbar, probably the same instrument they used on his splintered wooden sign. Hadn't they heard of a lock pick? Break in, but save the damn door. Bunch of neanderthals.

Ruby shook her head. She raised her arms high. "Well, good thing you're retiring."

Fernando looked past Ruby into his office and saw the damage. Everything he'd carefully packed in boxes this morning had been dumped out on the floor and then kicked to pieces. Papers, receipts, manila file folders, and worst of all the framed photos of Estelle and his two daughters he kept on the corner of his desk. Even his laptop had been thrown against the rear wall and lay open next to what had been his mini-refrigerator. The mini-fridge had been kicked apart and every remaining bottle of Modelo smashed on the floor, glass everywhere. The office reeked of Modelo. Destroying a man's beer supply. That was low.

Ruby came up behind him and put her hand on his shoulder, giving it a gentle squeeze. "Don't worry, we'll help you clean up. I'll get some of my ladies from he Co-op to help, if we need them."

Fernando nodded. "Thanks."

"I heard the racket from my gallery, but by the time I figured out where it was coming from and got down here, they were already leaving. A couple of guys in a black Toyota, scary looking bastards. I didn't try to stop them."

"No matter, I know who they are," Fernando said.

11

Now Fernando was involved, whether he wanted to be or not. That realization both depressed and angered him. A war with the Sinaloa Cartel was the last thing he needed now that he was finally trying to retire. He blamed Antonio for dragging him into this mess. And Lacy for his stubbornness. Why couldn't Lacy just give back the advance and be done with it? Why go to war over money he apparently didn't need?

Fernando's immediate problem was his office. He couldn't leave it like this, so he borrowed a broom and mop from Ruby and cleaned up the smashed bottles of Modelo, the broken glass and the puddles of beer. Then he gathered together all the files and papers on the floor, some of them soaked with beer, and stuffed them back in the two cardboard boxes: one box for what looked like business records, and the other for random crap. He'd planned to take both boxes back to his house, but after this he decided to save only the box with his business records. He took the box filled with crap outside and tossed it in the industrial dumpster behind Essentia next door. The only other thing he kept was his busted laptop. Maybe one of the computer repair shops could repair it or at least save some of the files on his hard drive, just in case he needed to access them in the future.

Exhausted, he collapsed in his desk chair and brooded, rehashing the events of the day in hopes of seeing a way out of his involvement in the Lacy-Archivada war. He'd been going to the dark place too often these days. Estelle said he was clinically depressed and needed medication. At one point last year he'd gone to the family doc and asked for an antidepressant, which he took for a week or so before flushing the rest down the toilet. All the meds did for him was numb the feeling and make his head feel like it was full of cotton. What Estelle and the family doc didn't understand was that he had damn good reasons for being depressed.

Just then Ruby walked in and looked around. "Wow! I can't believe you cleaned up the place so fast. I was just about to call the girls and ask for help. I might have to let you clean my gallery."

Fernando laughed. "Yeah, I couldn't just leave it like that. Just the sight of the mess pissed me off."

"Oh, hell, forget your troubles for a while," Ruby said. "We're late for Happy Hour."

Fernando checked his watch. "So it is. What was I thinking? By the way, where's your sister?"

"She went back to Abiquiu to burn all Andy's clothes!" Ruby said. "I told her to give them to Goodwill, but she said no, she wanted to see them burn and imagine Andy wearing them while they burned!"

Fernando laughed. "That's cold."

Ruby smiled and grabbed his arm. "Let's go."

It took him a while, but he managed to jimmy the damaged door to his office closed and just left it, unlocked and vulnerable. Nothing of value remained anyway. Then he followed Ruby down Canyon Road to El Farol, his favorite of the many historical buildings on Canyon Road. It was a great place to eat or drink, as everyone on Canyon Road could testify, especially the artists in the neighborhood, who usually skipped the eating.

As they approached the long porch in front Fernando noticed what appeared to be a homeless man sleeping at one of the outdoor tables on the patio. He shrugged, stepping up on the porch where a string of lights and red chile ristras hung from the ceiling of the porch, its beams and railings and window frames painted a dark brown color that contrasted with the tan stucco on the adobe.

Inside, a couple of old timers sat at the bar, nursing their beers, while Blaine Rogers, the owner of Picasso and Co. gallery, and Dave Stein, an 80-year-old painter, waved at them from a table in the restaurant part of El Farol. They sat in front of the brightly colored mural of Flamenco dancers on the rear wall as they did every afternoon at this time. The two of them were regular fixtures at El Farol, part of Canyon Road's artistic crowd who considered El Farol their second home.

Blaine waved them over, a big man wearing his usual red Bermuda shorts and a khaki fishing vest over a white T-shirt. At six feet, four inches tall and two hundred fifty pounds, Blaine was almost as big as Antonio, but with a hefty beer belly instead of bulging muscles. His long raven black hair fell into his eyes as he yelled across the room, "I saved you a place."

"Hah!" Ruby responded. "Nobody else would want to sit with you two drunks anyway."

Blaine and Ruby had known each other for years. Sometime friends, sometimes enemies, and occasionally lovers, the two were equally prickly and more than a few decibels too loud. They fought constantly.

"Don't get me started, Ruby, I'm in no mood for your insults today," Blaine said, pouring himself another glass of beer from his pitcher. The big man could drink all day and night.

Ruby sat next to Dave Stein, a wizened little man with olive skin that glowed and wisps of gray hair sticking up from various parts of his skull and out of his ears. He wore a blue suit that he'd worn for years and as far as anyone knew never took off. He rarely spoke, especially now that his long-time friend and fellow painter Wayne Fontenot had recently died, leaving him friendless, except for Blaine and Ruby, who usually ignored him while they bickered.

Fernando walked back to the bar and ordered a margarita for Ruby and a Modelo draft for himself. He carried the two drinks back to the table just in time to hear Blaine say, "Where's Tessa? She's hot!"

Ruby exploded. "Jesus, Blaine! Her husband's not even in the ground yet and you're hitting on her?"

"Life goes on, Ruby!" Blaine responded. "Remember Jimmy? You didn't waste any time after he was gone."

"He was my ex, you ass!" Ruby snapped.

Fernando turned away and took a big drink of his Modelo. He was used to tuning out the two of them. Blaine and Ruby could go on bickering for hours. The alcohol just loosened their tongues. On several occasions over the years the bickering had ended in a physical confrontation, with Ruby giving as good as she received and both of them getting thrown out of the restaurant and receiving week-long bans. Like a couple of juvenile delinquents at school.

While they bickered, the front door opened and in walked Manny carrying an Ipad of all things. He looked around the room, spotted them at the table, and made a beeline toward Fernando.

"Thought I might find you here," Manny said, out of breath. "We have a breakthrough in the Nageezi murder."

Fernando spun his chair around. "No kidding?"

"One of the news videographers at KRQE-TV in Albuquerque sent us a video," Manny said. "Turns out, the station sent a truck to Nageezi to cover the demonstration. The nightly anchor saw our announcement and passed it along to one of the video editors, who went through the film and found the footage. Wait 'till you see this."

Fernando tossed back the rest of his Modelo and stood.

"Let's go to the back corner, away from the windows," Manny said, leading Fernando to an empty table.

Manny waited until Fernando was seated and then loaded the

video. When he pushed the play button a fuzzy blur of colors appeared, then focused in on the highway overlooking the parking lot where the shooting occurred. To the right of the screen sat a large black vehicle, which Fernando recognized immediately as Siva Archivada's Range Rover. At first the image was somewhat out of focus, but as the camera zoomed in closer they saw a flash of light and a puff of smoke coming from the front window of the black vehicle.

Manny stopped the video there and backed it up. "Now watch this as I focus on the crowd."

Using his fingers, Manny enlarged the far left corner of the screen. It showed a young man dressed in a paramilitary uniform carrying an assault weapon. Suddenly the image blurs as someone steps in front of the man with the assault weapon. Fernando recognized that someone as Andy Dejon. Instantly Dejon's body jerks, staggers, and falls forward out of the picture.

"You see, the bullets were meant for the guy in the paramilitary uniform. Andy Dejon just happened to step in front of the guy and into the path of the bullets. It was an accident."

"So who was the intended victim?" Fernando asked.

"Well, that's the other thing," Manny said, shaking his head. "We sent the video to the FBI for identification. They think it's a member of the CJNG Cartel."

"Never heard of it," Fernando said.

"You will, they're a relatively new cartel but getting stronger," Manny said. "The Cartel Jalisco Nueva Generacion. They're competing with the Sinaloa Cartel in Mexico and increasingly here in the Southwest. They've moved into Phoenix and El Paso and are starting to appear in Albuquerque. You can identify them by their military uniforms, that's their calling card. They pose as regular Mexican military, they even carry the same assault rifle used by the military: the FX-05 Xiuhcoatl, the so-called 'Fire Serpent.' Their leader is a guy they call 'El Mencho.' His real name is Nemesio Cervantes. He's Silva Archivada's arch enemy."

Fernando frowned, not happy to hear about this second cartel. One cartel was one too many. Two would mean big trouble because the cartels would be competing. "So we're about to have a cartel war here, is that what you're saying?"

"I'm afraid that's what it looks like it," Manny said. "And the CJNG Cartel is supposedly more ruthless than the Sinaloa. They have to be to compete with Sinaloa, which is already established in these cities."

Then Fernando noticed Ruby standing behind them listening. "Did you hear the news?"

"Yeah, I heard," Ruby said, backing away. "I'll tell Tessa that Andy's shooting was an accident. Not that it makes much difference, but it might make her feel better to know that it wasn't one of the angry husbands who killed Andy."

"Yeah, just bad luck," Fernando said, shaking his head.

Ruby nodded. "You can say that again. Andy was bad luck from the first time Tessa saw him."

12

Fernando awoke to what sounded like the chatter of television news. At first he thought he was dreaming, then he realized that Estelle must have the television on in the living room. Something big must have happened. Estelle hated the television. She never watched the boob tube except for the nightly PBS News, sometimes not even that. What now? Suddenly he feared another national tragedy like 9/11 had occurred. Or maybe it could be something local, like the assassination of a prominent Santa Fean at the hands of Jack Lacy?

He crawled out of bed, splashed cold water on his face, slipped on a pair of jeans, and hobbled barefoot down the hallway to the living room. He found Estelle fully dressed for work sitting on the sofa watching a special bulletin on one of the local stations. Looked like a large fire with lots of smoke and a large police presence around the circumference of the property. The location looked vaguely familiar, although the thick smoke obscured most of the burning building. The on-the-scene reporter stood off to the side interviewing a witness, a bystander who was describing what she'd seen when the fire exploded in the building.

Estelle turned to him and said, "Somebody fire-bombed that old Line Camp Saloon in Pojoaque early this morning."

"What? You're sure?" Fernando muttered, still not fully awake. He hurried to the sofa and sat beside Estelle. They listened to the reporter summarize what authorities knew so far: that the former Line Camp Saloon had been totally destroyed by what was being called a fire bomb and that one person's remains, as yet unidentified, had been found in the ruins.

Fernando, confused, went to the kitchen and poured himself a cup of coffee. His mind began to race as he drank the coffee, trying to make sense of this turn of events. His first thought was that Jack Lacy had started the fire to strike Silva Archivada first, before the Sinaloa Cartel could strike him. That was a possibility, except Lacy was a sniper and not a firebomber, at least as far as he knew. Then he remembered what Manny had said about the rival cartel competing with Sinaloa and the video Manny had shown him of the shooting in Nageezi. A Sinaloa gunman had tried to take out a member of the new CJNG Cartel and failed. It made sense that the CJNG Cartel would be looking for revenge against Sinaloa. So maybe the cartel war had started.

Troubled, Fernando took his coffee into his study and called Manny. Manny answered on the first ring.

"Do you see what's going on in Pojoaque?" Fernando asked.

"I'm watching it too," Manny said. "I don't know any more than you do. Probably less, because I just turned on the television."

"Are you on your way out there?"

Manny laughed. "I'm trying to wake up, I haven't left for work yet. But no, I'm not going out there. Pojoaque is out of my jurisdiction. That's the county's problem, not mine. I imagine the sheriff's already there...or on her way."

That caused Fernando to pause. "Her?"

"Yeah...you do know that your friend Jodie Williams was appointed sheriff, after Apodaca retired, right?" Manny asked. "I don't know if it's a temporary or permanent appointment."

"Maybe I did hear something about that," Fernando said, trying to remember. "I'm not surprised. She's a damn good cop."

Manny agreed. "Yes she is."

"Do you think Lacy could be involved in this firebombing?"

"How would I know?" Manny shot back.

"Okay, sorry to bother you," Fernando said and clicked off.

Not satisfied, Fernando tried calling Antonio but didn't get an answer. He figured Antonio was probably out on his morning run. The big man didn't own a television, living as he did in a cabin out in the Pecos Wilderness. Antonio liked his solitude and his simple pleasures. He probably wasn't even aware of what had happened this morning in Pojoaque.

Finally curiosity got the better of Fernando. He decided to go out to Pojoaque himself to check out the fire scene, maybe talk to Jodie Williams if she happened to be there. He dressed quickly, wolfed down a piece of toast and jam with a second cup of coffee, and then said goodbye to Estelle, who sat transfixed in front of their television sipping her morning coffee. This marked the first morning in weeks that he had left the house before Estelle.

He drove around the Paseo to Highway 84/285 and cruised through the green hills sparkling in the morning sun as he passed the Santa Fe

Opera. Approaching Buffalo Thunder on the Pojoaque strip he could see black smoke rising up from the fire scene straight ahead. The black smoke dissolved in the thin mountain air like drops of blood in water. Only one red fire truck remained, still pumping water on the smoldering remains of what was once the Line Camp Saloon and more recently Heaven's Door. He also saw two Santa Fe Country Sheriff's cruisers and an ambulance. A crowd of onlookers brought up the rear, forming a loose semi circle around the fire scene. Must have been at least twenty or thirty people.

Fernando drove past the crowd, noticing all their cars scattered along the shoulder of the highway. He pulled over next to a bone-dry arroyo filled with trash and empty beer cans. He locked the Cherokee, leaving his Smith & Wesson in the glove department, and walked back to where the crowd had gathered. He noticed Deputy Sheriff John Rodriguez working crowd control, trying to keep the crowd back away from the smoldering fire. He remembered John from their raid on Three Hills Ranch, where Robert Warner ran a sex ranch trafficking young women to old pedophiles from the West Coast. He hadn't seen John since that fateful day, the day Warner died in a fiery helicopter crash while trying to escape.

"John!" Fernando yelled and waved, squeezing through the crowd to reach the deputy.

John turned and waved when he saw who'd called out to him. "Fernando–what are you doing here?"

"I'm on an investigation," Fernando said, stretching the truth a bit. He couldn't explain what he was doing because he didn't know himself. "Is Jodie here?"

"Yeah, she's inside the house talking to the owner," John said, pointing to a casita behind the burned out building, next to a smaller building that looked like some sort of shed or barn.

"Thanks," Fernando said. He made his way around the smoldering ruin, keeping his distance to avoid the intense heat still radiating from the rubble. The door of the small adobe casita hung wide open. Inside he saw Jodie standing in the hallway talking to Archivada, who sat on a sofa with his legs crossed, looking as imperious as ever. Jodie looked like she'd put on a few pounds, which just made her look more muscular. Tall, athletic, with short-cropped dark hair, she had been a star player on the University of New Mexico's women's basketball team. A real jock. Watching her now, he didn't doubt she could still play.

Fernando eased up to the door and then stopped, not sure if he should intrude on their discussion. Finally he knocked on the door and stepped inside. Jodie turned to look at him, hand on her service revolver. "Fernando, I didn't expect to see you here," Jodie said.

"On a case," Fernando replied simply.

Archivada nodded from the sofa. "You see, Mister Lopez, this is what happens when I try to run a legitimate business. What am I to do?"

Jodie looked puzzled. "You two know each other?"

"Oh, yes, we've had our moments," Fernando said, not wanting to get into specifics. His connection to Archivada was not something he could explain quickly, if at all.

Jodie gave Fernando a dirty look and then turned back to Archivada. "So you were saying you know who did this, who firebombed your business?"

"Yes, of course we know who did this," Archivada said. 'The Jalisco Nueva Generacion Cartel. They want to take over my business, and look what they do." He opened his arms wide, as if to show Fernando and Jodie. "These people, this El Mencho, is nothing but a butcher, a murderer. He is not a businessman like myself, he just wants to torture and murder and give orders like a dictator. If he take over, he turn the land into a slaughterhouse. Like he kill Leroy this morning, my lieutenant."

Through the back windows Fernando noticed a large vehicle pulling up beside the casita, a black Toyota Sequoia with three rows of seats. A total of eight shadowy figures climbed out of the Sequoia, several of them wearing hooded sweatshirts. They milled around for a few seconds and then headed for the out building, whatever it was. Looked like the troops were gathering. That meant more trouble. A full-blown cartel war seemed immanent.

Jodie stared at Archivada, skeptical. "So where can we find this El Mencho? Do you know where these people are based?"

"Maybe yes, maybe no," Archivada responded. "They move around, one safe house after another. They have lots of safe houses in Albuquerque. I think not as many in Santa Fe, I don't know."

"Give us a moment, will you?" Jodie said to Fernando.

Fernando took the hint. He stepped outside and eyed the crowd, looking for troublemakers as a way of helping John. Given his mood, they all looked like troublemakers.

A few minutes later Jodie walked outside and approached Fernando. "We need to talk," she said, pointing toward Santa Fe. "Meet me at the McDonalds down the road in thirty minutes, okay?"

Fernando saluted and watched as Jodie made her way through the crowd to John. He noticed the crowd was beginning to thin out, losing interest in the carnage now that the flames were all but extinguished.

Glad to be leaving the stench of the fire, Fernando hiked back to where he left his Cherokee. He deliberated a few moments before pulling out onto the highway. Since he had thirty minutes to kill, he stopped first at Buffalo Thunder and walked through the huge casino that both amused and depressed him. What a portrait of humanity! Poor people gambling away what little money they had. He wondered if all casinos were as depressing.

One walk-through was enough, thank you. He climbed back into the Cherokee and drove down the road to the McDonalds. Jody hadn't arrived yet, so he walked into the McDonalds, ordered an iced tea, and found a booth for them overlooking the highway.

Jodie arrived momentarily. She bought a Diet Coke at the counter and joined him in the booth. "Okay, so what's your involvement in all this?" she asked, as abruptly as always. Jodie was not one to waste words.

Fernando leaned back in the booth and sighed. He told her about Jack Lacy and the information Lacy provided concerning the proposed hit on Dee Highland at Chaco Canyon. He explained that when the hit had to be called off because of the protests at Chaco, Lacy's employer demanded Lacy return a two hundred and fifty thousand dollar advance, which Lacy refused to do. In response, Lacy's employer contracted with Silva Archivada and the Sinaloa Cartel to get the advance back, whatever it took.

Jodie looked puzzled. "Okay, but what does all this have to do with you? What's your connection?"

"I blame Antonio," Fernando said, shaking his head. "Turns out Antonio and Lacy were in the same Marine unit in Iraq. They're old war buddies and apparently good friends. So good that Antonio felt he had to resign from the Santa Fe Police Department out of loyalty, so that he wouldn't have to go after Lacy. Then he asked for my help with Lacy. I don't know what the hell he expects me to do, or how I can help, but that's the long and short of it."

Jodie frowned, not pleased. "We got the notice about Lacy in Santa Fe, but the rest of this is news to me. "Lacy was actually going to assassinate Dee Highland? Jesus Christ!"

"That's what he claims," Fernando said, "and after seeing him, I have no reason to doubt him. He's a pretty damn imposing figure."

"So I gather from his reputation," Jodie said and then motioned back toward the scene of the fire. "What do you know about this firebombing? Have you heard of this other cartel that Archivada claims is responsible?"

Fernando relayed what Manny had told him about the Cartel Jalisco Nueva Generacion, CJNG for short. "Manny says they're moving into the American Southwest competing with Sinaloa. He says they're already in El Paso and Albuquerque and headed north."

Jodie shook her head. "That's the last thing I wanted to hear."

"You saw the vehicle pull up behind the house back there, right? Looked like Archivada was gathering his troops to return the favor on the CJING."

"Yeah, I saw them," Jodie said. "I don't like this, not one bit. A cartel war right here In Santa Fe? We have enough problems already."

"I hear you," Fernando said. "I feel bad for Manny. Without Antonio, he won't get much support down at the Washington Avenue Station."

"We're not in a much better position to help," Jodie said. "I can't even staff our usual patrols we're so short-handed. Nobody wants to be a cop anymore. Too dangerous."

"Can you blame them?" Fernando asked.

The question lingered in the air as they sat in silence, staring out the window, wondering what Archivada was planning to do next.

13

Ironically, Fernando had finally made some progress in retiring, thanks to Archivada's thugs. Not much was left in his office to save after they'd finished their dirty work. That morning he'd taken his beloved MacBook to the computer shop and, lo and behold, the technicians had managed to repair the damaged laptop by replacing the battery and several other parts. They'd shown him a laundry list of the parts they'd replaced, but he didn't know what the hell they were talking about or how the miniscule parts functioned. So he just nodded and pretended he understood and then handed over his credit card. Everyone was happy.

After an early lunch, he'd spent the better part of the afternoon deleting hundreds of files from his laptop. Now he sat at his desk wondering if he should record a new message on his battered but working answering machine that informed callers that he was no longer in business. Or maybe eliminate the phone line altogether. That might make more sense. Why pay for a phone line when the business was now defunct or soon to be defunct?

The buzzing of his cell phone ended his ruminations. He picked up the phone and answered when he saw the name on the screen.

"It didn't take them long," Jodie responded.

"What do you mean?" Fernando asked, fearing the worst, given the tone of her voice.

"Archivada and the Sinaloa Cartel," Jodie said. "They hit a Jalisco safe house near La Cienega a couple of hours ago. Manny's there now. I guess it's not a pretty sight."

Fernando sighed. "Manny better watch out. He got the worst of it the last time he tangled with the Sinaloa crowd. I hope he's there with backup."

"Sounds like it," Jodie said, reassuring Fernando.

"Where is this place?" Fernando asked.

"It's on County Road fifty-four heading Southwest toward La

Bajada," Jodie said. "Manny said it was an old abandoned farm between the Santa Fe River and La Cienega Creek."

"Are you on your way there now?" Fernando asked.

"No, I have a situation out in Eldorado. Hit and run, one critically injured woman. I'm waiting for the ambulance now. If you go, let me know what you find out," Jodie said, clicking off.

Fernando knew he shouldn't go because it was none of his business, but he couldn't leave Manny out there without knowing for sure he had sufficient backup. Not after what had happened to him the last time they'd had a shootout with Sinaloa. He debated whether to stop by his house on the way and pick up his Steyr sniper rifle, but decided against it to save time. The Smith & Wesson would have to do, so he buckled on his holster before leaving.

Fernando closed up shop, locking his office door and driving down to the Paseo and around to Old Santa Fe Trail, which he took to I-25 South, the fastest way to get to La Cienega. He shot down the interstate to Entrada La Cienega and drove up to County Road 54 and turned left, heading toward La Bajada. The old road skirted along La Cienega Creek, over the smoky green mesa. Less than a mile down the road he saw the police action straight ahead, two cruisers and a forensics van gathered on a small hill overlooking the creek.

Fernando relaxed. At least it looked like Manny had adequate backup for whatever the situation was at the abandoned farm. He turned into a winding dirt drive that curved up to the top of the hill. He first came to an old Dodge minivan with its front and side windows blasted out and its doors riddled with bullet holes. A dead man wearing a military uniform was sprawled out of the driver's seat, half in and half out of the van. The dead man's chest was a massive open wound dripping into a large puddle of reddish-brown blood pooled on the driveway below.

Fernando continued on toward the farmhouse, a ramshackle frame building with white siding starting to turn gray and a long veranda in front supported by large rocks the size of small boulders. Behind the house he saw a series of empty corrals in varying degrees of disrepair and a large fenced-in garden overrun with weeds. Further back the remains of a small barn teetered on the brink of collapse. Part of its roof had already imploded, leaving a black, gaping hole. Looked like the farm had been abandoned for quite a few years.

Manny stood in the front yard talking to Miguel of Forensics. A couple of other cops were searching the back yard. Both Manny and Miguel waved as Fernando pulled off to the side of the driveway, keeping his distance. He didn't want to disturb any evidence.

Stepping out of the Cherokee, Fernando spotted two more bodies over by the front door to the farmhouse. Like the dead man in the Dodge van, the two of them wore military fatigues.

Fernando shook his head. "Quite a scene."

Manny chuckled. "Yeah, Sinaloa can sure leave a mess behind for others to clean up. We're gonna be here all week."

"This is nothing," Miguel said, opening his arms. "You should see the scene inside. Four more dead, blood everywhere. And there's another one out back that Teresa is examining. Poor fucker tried to run for the hills. Looks like he was hit in the back by a bazooka!"

Fernando nodded. "You think any of them got away to continue the war?" he asked Manny.

"Don't know, maybe," Manny said. "We found tire tracks of several vehicles, so maybe some of the Jalisco Cartel either weren't here or managed to get away before the fire-fight erupted."

Fernando glanced at the tire tracks crisscrossing the driveway.

"But don't worry, they'll be back," Manny said. "If you see one, then there's likely more on the way."

Fernando considered. "What about the Sinaloa Cartel? Do you have any idea where they relocated after the firebombing in Pojoaque? When I was talking to Jodie at the fire we saw eight of them arrive in a black Toyota Sequoia. They must be holed up somewhere in Santa Fe."

Manny shook his head. "No idea. We haven't received any reports or complaints from neighbors, nothing. If they have other safe houses in the area, we don't know where they're located."

"Well, shit," Fernando said, kicking at the dirt in the driveway. "I suppose if there are any Jalisco left, we'll see more of this."

"Maybe," Manny said, "although they're new to the area, they don't have the manpower Sinaloa has, according to what we've been told. At least for the time being anyway."

"Let's hope," Fernando said, turning away. Then he stopped and turned back to Manny. "Come to think of it, Archivada bought that old Forest Service building on Upper Canyon Road, where we had the shootout. At least he claimed he was buying that building back when he bought the old Line Camp and was claiming to be a legitimate businessman."

"Yeah, well, fuck that!" Manny said. "I'm not going near that place, that's where I almost died. Losing a kidney...and six weeks in the hospital... no thank you! I'll resign first. Sometimes I think I should have resigned back then when I woke up in that recovery room."

"I don't think anyone would blame you," Fernando said.

Manny, shaking his head, followed Miguel back to the house.

Fernando walked slowly back to his Cherokee, trying to decide what to do next. He climbed into the Cherokee and drove back to I-25. He got off the interstate at the Old Santa Fe Trail and took the Paseo to Canyon Road. Against his better judgment, he drove past his office and soon found himself on Upper Canyon Road. He passed the alley leading to the run-down adobe where Wayne Fontenot had lived, an old painter who had been a regular at the El Farol Happy Hours with Ruby and the other artistic types on Canyon Road until his death last year. He and Ruby had taken care of Wayne the last few months of his life. Funny, Fernando missed the old bastard, even though Wayne had been difficult at the end, suffering from dementia. Pretty much by himself Wayne had created the Devil on Canyon Road hysteria last year. Thinking about Wayne, Fernando had to smile.

Upper Canyon Road ended at the aging Forest Service building, a two-story log A-frame with a wrap-around porch, its logs discolored by black mold and wood rot in spots. Approaching the A-frame, surrounded on three sides by the National Forest, Fernando saw 'No Trespassing' signs on both sides of the road. The signs were new. He didn't remember any signs on the road before. He slowed down, trying to get a read on what, if anything, was going on at the building. Then he saw the black Toyota Sequoia parked off to the side of the A-frame. Bingo!

So he'd been right. The Sinaloa Cartel bought the building as one of their safe houses, just as Archivada had said.

Fernando slowed to a stop in the center of the parking lot, where Silva's men shot Manny last year. He didn't want to revisit that nightmare. Still, he made no move to leave, studying the A-frame for signs of activity. He saw nothing at first, no one outside anyway.

Suddenly the front door swung open. Then a short, stocky man turned two Doberman loose. The dogs ran lickety-split to the Cherokee. Snarling and barking, the huge beasts jumped against the fenders and on the hood, trying to rip through the windows with their teeth.

Fernando froze, paralyzed with fear. He hated vicious dogs with a passion, ever since he'd been attacked by a pack of wild dogs when he was twelve years old. The fear of growling dogs and slashing teeth had never left him.

It took all his strength to force himself to move. He threw the Cherokee in gear and hit the gas pedal hard. The Cherokee spun around in the loose dirt, flinging off the dogs. Then he squealed across the parking lot, heading toward the road, just as he heard the one sound he didn't want to hear.

Thok! Thok!

The bullets shattered the rear window and showered Fernando with fragments of glass. Stung like hell.

Fernando struggled to keep the Cherokee on the road. Then he noticed his hands on the wheel were bleeding. He wiped them on his jeans and kept driving, barreling down the dirt road and onto Canyon Road. He glanced in the rear view mirror to see if the Toyota Sequoia was following him. It wasn't.

Relieved, Fernando eased up on the gas pedal and cruised down to the Paseo and over to Acequia Madre. He'd had enough for today. Besides, he needed to clean up before Estelle came home. He didn't want her to see him like this. No way. What she didn't know wouldn't kill her.

It might kill him, but not Estelle.

14

His immediate problem, Fernando realized, was the shattered rear window of his Cherokee. He parked the Cherokee off to the side of their garage near a stand of cottonwood trees, hoping Estelle wouldn't notice the window at that distance. First thing tomorrow he would drive to his favorite auto glass shop on Cerrillos Road and have them replace the window, as they had done for at least one window of every car he'd ever owned. Went with the job.

Unfortunately, Estelle spotted the damage as she drove her Camry into the garage. "What happened to your rear window?" she said as she walked through the patio door and saw him sitting at the kitchen table drinking a Modelo.

Fernando shook his head, trying to think of an explanation that would seem at least remotely feasible. "Uh, well, one of those plumber's trucks with the pipes hanging over its roof ran into the rear of my Cherokee. Busted out the rear window."

That was the best he could do. Not good enough.

Estelle gave him the Evil Eye. "Uh-huh." She started to say something but then stopped herself. Don't ask, don't tell had been their policy for the last few years. Worked for both of them.

Fernando spent most of the next morning at the auto glass store, fidgeting and pacing in the waiting room while the technicians worked to find and install a new rear window in the Cherokee. The technicians got tired of him pestering them every fifteen minutes and asked him to have a seat in the waiting room. Instead, he went outside and sat on a bench and tried to meditate if for no other reason than to lower his blood pressure. Seemed like one long, forty-eight hour day, like yesterday never ended. By the time he pulled out on Cerrillos Road with a brand new rear window it was nearly Noon. The day was half over, wasted.

As always he drove on automatic pilot to his office. Ruby was just getting into her Honda Accord when he climbed out of the Cherokee. He noticed both halves of his Private Eye sign were lying in the dust now. He picked them up and carried them behind Essentia to the dumpster. One toss and they were gone. He was a free man. Officially retired.

On his way back to the Cherokee he found Ruby waving at him to get his attention. "Manny stopped by looking for you. He wants you to call him as soon as possible."

Fernando waved back. "Okay," he shouted.

Now what? Had Archivada made a move on Jack Lacy...or had Lacy made a move on Archivada? Or was it another battle in the cartel wars? He couldn't keep track of all that was going on.

Fernando walked down the gravel path to his office. He noticed that Ruby had repaired the door. Same lock, fortunately, so he unlocked the door and walked into his empty office and took a seat at his empty desk. The place no longer even looked like an office, so why was he here? Why did he drive down every morning on automatic pilot? He started to feel ridiculous.

Shaking off the self-examination, he called Manny on his cell phone.

"Fernando, I'm glad you called," Manny answered. "I've got some news."

"Yeah? What's up?" Fernando said, and leaned back in his chair, expecting the worst.

"It's Lacy," Manny said. "Turns out he has these bouts of paranoia or something like paranoia, I don't know what to call it. He went crazy last night in La Fonda and got kicked out. They want him gone by the end of the day."

"What do you mean he went crazy?" Fernando asked.

"Crazy bastard was raving in the hallway, waving a gun and saying someone was walking back and forth outside his door stalking him, someone wearing a long black coat," Manny said. "That's what I mean by crazy."

Fernando laughed. "Sounds like the ghost story of the tall man in the long black coat walking the hallways of La Fonda. The local paranormals claim to have recorded several sightings."

"Yeah, well, that's another thing," Manny said. "Lacy says he attracts ghosts, that they pursue him."

Fernando did not respond. How did you respond to a statement like that?

"You hear?" Manny asked, exasperated. "He says he sees ghosts and they follow him, something like that."

"I heard you," Fernando said finally.

"Antonio's with Lacy now, trying to calm him down," Manny said. "He wanted me to call you and see if you would give him a hand."

"Great!" Fernando said and clicked off. He tossed his cell phone on the desk. How did he ever get involved in such craziness?

Disgusted, he pocketed his cell phone, locked up his office, and headed downtown. He parked on Alameda, as he always did, being a self-acknowledged OCD candidate. OCD was the least of his problems.

When Fernando walked into the front lobby of La Fonda, Fred Mondragon who managed the hotel waved. Fred came out from behind the counter, a small man wearing a tan suit with a necktie as white as his hair. Fred looked worried.

"Fernando, you gotta get this Lacy guy out of the hotel," Fred said. "He's disturbing the other guests. He's nuts!"

Fernando laughed. "I guess so. Is Antonio with him now?"

Fred nodded and pointed across the way to La Plazuela, the first-floor restaurant. Antonio and Lacy were sitting at one of the front tables, on display to everyone in the restaurant and lobby. As before, Lacy wore black from head to foot. Even his open carry holster was black.

Antonio waved from the table with a hang-dog expression on his face. Looked nervous, like he could use some help.

Fernando walked across the lobby and pulled up a chair. He sat directly across from Lacy, who kept glancing around, as though looking for someone. Or a way to get out of there fast.

"Hey, Jack...are you okay?" Fernando asked after he sat down, not very sympathetically.

"We're a little stressed right now," Antonio said. "They want us to leave right after we finish lunch. We're still waiting to order. I don't know what's taking them so long."

Fernando noticed the sweat beading on Lacy's forehead. Not a good sign. Why would Antonio bring Lacy to La Plazuela, one of the most haunted spots in Santa Fe, if Lacy was so afraid of ghosts? It didn't figure. Everyone in Santa Fe was familiar with the La Fonda ghost stories, including the company man who gambled away his company's money and then committed suicide by jumping into a well once located in the center of today's La Plazuela.

Lacy's eyes darted from Antonio to Fernando and back to Antonio, a time bomb waiting to explode.

"So what's the problem?" Fernando asked, out of patience.

"Too many ghosts here, that's the problem," Lacy said out of the corner of his mouth. "They find me, they follow me. I can't get away from them."

"Ghosts," Fernando said, mostly to himself. "Why you? Why do they follow you?"

"Because I see them, I've walked with them," Lacy said, his eyes flashing. "They're just shades. They can't harm anyone, and yet they remind you...."

"Of what?" Fernando asked, starting to lose his patience, what little patience he had left.

"Okay, so we need to get you to a safer, quieter place," Antonio interrupted, changing the subject. "Maybe you'd like to stay in my cabin for a while, what do you say to that? Pecos is off grid, you might like it."

Lacy stared at Antonio, saying nothing.

"Then maybe we could look around town and find you a quiet Inn or a casita to rent for as long as you're in Santa Fe," Antonio continued. "You could check it out first, just to make sure you aren't getting yourself in another situation with...you know, ghosts."

Suddenly Lacy stood up, knocking his chair backwards. The crashing chair echoed in the packed room. "No, get away from me!" Lacy shouted. "Leave me alone!"

Everyone in La Plazuela stared at Lacy.

"What do you want?" Lacy shouted, across the room.

Very quickly two beefy security guards wearing matching blue blazers and gray slacks descended on the table. "Mister Mondragon wants you out of the hotel–now!" the bigger of the two barked. His nametag identified him as Dale. "We'll help you collect your things and leave." He reached out and touched Lacy's arm.

"Touch me again and I'll kill you," Lacy hissed between clenched teeth.

Dale glanced at his companion, Tom, who was older and not quite as big.

Then Tom stepped up to diffuse the situation. "Follow us to your room, we'll give you a hand," he said cheerfully. He turned and led the way through the tables in La Plazuela into the lobby to the elevator. He held the elevator door open for the rest of the entourage. Fernando and Antonio followed, with Lacy bringing up the rear, tentatively following.

They disembarked on the third floor. Again Tom led the way, opening the door to Lacy's room and leading them inside. Dale and Tom began to gather Lacy's belongings, placing his suitcase on the king size bed and laying his clothes alongside. Then Tom made the mistake of grabbing Lacy's gun case in the closet. Lacy jumped, reaching for his open carry holster.

Tom reacted quickly. "Whoa, why don't we let you take care of that item," he said, moving slowly, carefully away from the closet.

Lacy grabbed the gun case and glared at the two security guards.

Fernando and Antonio stood back and watched Tom and Dale work. Lacy helped after a while, placing his clothing carefully in the suitcase and then zipping it closed. When they finished packing, Dale took the suitcase and let Lacy carry his gun case out of the room, down the stairs, and across the lobby to Antonio's Wrangler in the parking garage.

"Thank you," Fred Mondragon whispered to Fernando as the procession walked by.

Antonio threw open the rear compartment of the Wrangler for the suitcase. Lacy stood back and watched the others work. Only when Tom and Dale moved back after loading the suitcase did Lacy step forward and place his gun case carefully next to the suitcase.

"You boys have a good day," Tom said, cheerfully. Dale glared at Antonio and Lacy as they climbed into the Wrangler.

Fernando moved back to the garage door, giving Antonio room to maneuver the big vehicle. "We'll meet you at my cabin in the Pecos," Antonio yelled out the window as he drove off.

"Why? What for?" Fernando yelled back. The question hung in the air as the Wrangler turned right on Cathedral Place and disappeared around the corner, heading for Pecos.

"Crazy motherfucker," Dale said to Fernando.

Then Tom and Dale walked back into La Fonda, leaving Fernando standing in the garage trying to make sense of what had just happened. Finally he gave up and headed for the Cherokee.

15

As he walked along Cathedral Place Fernando debated what to do next. Antonio assumed he would be willing to follow them to Pecos. Talk about presumptuous. Why in the world would he want to meet them at Antonio's cabin? What could he possibly do to help Antonio out of an impossible situation that Antonio, after all, had created for himself? Fernando could think of a dozen reasons not to drive all the way out to Pecos to meet them and not one damn reason to actually do it. He was, after all, supposed to be retired.

Brooding, he walked over to Alameda Street and sat on one of the benches along the Santa Fe River to think. Antonio had come unglued since Jack Lacy arrived in town. Not only had Antonio resigned from the Santa Fe Police Department, a job he was extremely good at, he spent every day escorting Lacy around town like some sort of chauffeur or personal servant. Lacy was the problem. There had to be a way to get rid of Lacy short of feeding him to Silva Archivada and the Sinaloa Cartel. Which, come to think of it, might not be such a bad idea.

Problem was, he wasn't a quitter. Never had been. He couldn't just walk away and not help Antonio in his time of need. So against his better judgment, he climbed into his Cherokee and drove up to the Paseo and over to Old Santa Fe Trail, which fed into the Old Las Vegas Highway heading east. Past I-25 the landscape changed: old city adobes gave way to sprawling subdivisions of frame and stucco houses, their lots manicured to picture perfect perfection. Only when he approached Bobcat Bite did the Santa Fe National Forest provide relief from the suburban sprawl. He slowed down when he passed Bobcat Bite, enjoying the scenery.

Soon he drove past the tiny village of Glorieta and began looking for the forest road that headed north toward La Cueva, an even smaller village. The driveway to Antonio's cabin branched off this forest road, about a hundred yards or so north of the highway. Moments later he spotted the forest road up ahead and turned left onto the road. Topping a small rise Fernando saw Antonio's long driveway below on the left, an unmaintained dirt road that ran like a ribbon into the tall ponderosa pines at the end of the drive.

Fernando slowed to a crawl as he continued on down the bumpy drive to Antonio's cabin: a small L-shaped log cabin that Antonio had purchased in Durango as a kit and then assembled by himself with a little help from a couple of fishing buddies who lived nearby. The cabin was built like a fortress, with a steel front door and iron bars over its windows. Antonio was a man who valued his privacy as much as Jack Lacy valued his. Fernando began to see that the two old war buddies were a lot more alike than he at first thought.

Up ahead the surrounding Ponderosa pines dwarfed the cabin. He parked behind Antonio's Wrangler and climbed out of his Cherokee. The crisp mountain air smelled fragrant with the scent of pine and something else, sage maybe. Though he would never want to live so far out of town, he had to admit it was a damn beautiful location at the edge of the national forest. Perfect for Antonio, who needed a quiet refuge after his time in Iraq and a turbulent marriage.

Fernando heard Antonio mumbling something to himself as he opened the door to the cabin. When he stepped inside, he found Antonio sitting in his leather recliner, the one and only extravagance he allowed himself in his otherwise Spartan lifestyle. The cabin was exactly the way Antonio wanted it: small and primitive. A couple of small tables and a bookcase completed his living area. The so-called kitchen had a wood burning stove and a heavy-duty REI cooler on the counter. With no electricity, Antonio depended on battery-operated Coleman lanterns. He had a solar panel on the roof to charge his cell phone and recharge his batteries. The bathroom consisted of a wooden outhouse out back behind the cabin.

"Where's Lacy?" Fernando asked.

Antonio raised his thumb over his shoulder. "He's out back using the facilities. You should have heard him complain when I told him I had no running water or electricity."

"Not much for roughing it, eh?" Fernando asked, taking a seat on one of the handmade wooden chairs. Fortunately the chair came with a seat cushion, which made sitting on it tolerable, if not comfortable. He wondered how Lacy was going to react to these less than palatial accommodations. Apparently the man in black enjoyed a celebrity lifestyle.

They heard Lacy cursing outside as he walked around the side of the cabin to the front door.

"Tony," Lacy said, frowning as though he was a bearer of bad news when he stepped through the door. He wiped his hands on his black slacks. "You can't be serious. I can't stay here–this is like camping, or worse, living in a shithole Third World country. I swore I'd never go camping again when I left Iraq. I'm used to staying in five-star resorts with all the luxuries I require. I'm a very rich man. I thought you understood that."

Antonio shrugged. "What can I say? This is how I choose to live. It helps me with my Post Traumatic Stress Disorder."

Fernando noticed a note of exasperation in Antonio's voice. Maybe the big man had reached his limit and was getting tired of babysitting Lacy and being treated like a servant. About time.

Lacy looked around the cabin. "Anyway, where would I sleep?"

"I have an extra cot in the bedroom. We could set it up out here to give you more privacy."

Lacy shook his head. "I can't sleep on a fucking cot. I need a king size bed and a clean, well-lighted place, like the Hemingway story says. I have trouble sleeping, just like you do. I need to leave the lights on in the hall or an adjacent room and to have classical music playing low on an FM radio station nearby. That's my routine. The only way I can get to sleep."

Neither Antonio nor Fernando responded or needed to respond. It was pretty obvious that Lacy wasn't going to find that here.

"So I'm going to have to find a five-stair hotel or resort somewhere in Santa Fe," Lacy said, perking up. "To do that I'll need a car, a fast car. Is there a BMW dealership in town?"

"Yes," Fernando answered. "Santa Fe BMW on Camino Entrada. It's easy to find–just off Cerrillos Road, south of Rodeo Road."

"Good," Lacy said, looking at his watch. "Can one of you drop me off. I'll take my bag with me. I won't be coming back here." Lacy looked around the room with noticeable disgust.

Fernando studied Antonio, who looked pissed, insulted by someone he considered a friend.

Feeling the bad vibes between the two men, Fernando decided to intervene in order to prevent Iraq War III. "Sure, I can drop you off on my way back to my office, no problem. Just say when."

"When," Lacy said, without hesitation. He grabbed his suitcase and gun case and then abruptly walked out of the cabin, leaving Antonio stunned.

"Don't worry about it, he's an asshole," Fernando said, noticing that Antonio's face had turned red with anger. "I'll take care of it."

Antonio nodded, still furious.

Fernando walked outside to find Lacy loading his bags in the rear compartment of the Cherokee. Not waiting for an invitation, Lacy climbed into the passenger's seat and buckled up. Fernando followed without speaking. He hit the ignition and eased into the driveway, noting that Antonio did not even come to the door of the cabin to see them off. Maybe the big man was rethinking his allegiance to Lacy.

"So you think Tony's going to be all right out here?" Lacy asked after a long, awkward silence. "What a shithole!"

Fernando pulled out of the driveway onto the forest road and headed for the Old Las Vegas Highway. He shrugged. "It's what Antonio likes. Not my cup of tea...and I guess not yours either."

More awkward silence as Fernando turned onto the Old Las Vegas Highway west toward Santa Fe. "We'll need to find you a place to stay, a new hotel or resort," Fernando said, trying to think of the quickest way to get rid of Lacy. He ran through a list of Santa Fe resorts in his mind.

"It needs to be someplace remote," Lacy responded, as usual talking out of the corner of his mouth, as if he were confiding a secret. "Either in the mountains or somewhere out of the way in the city. Somewhere away from the crowd, where I can be anonymous."

"With all the luxuries you require," Fernando added, not bothering to hide his sarcasm.

Lacy glanced at Fernando. "I have my standards."

Suddenly the ideal place for Lacy occurred to him: Bishop's Lodge, an exclusive, over-the-top resort between Santa Fe and Tesuque that bordered the Santa Fe National Forest.

"I know the perfect place," Fernando said. "It's outside Santa Fe on the road to Tesuque, a four-hundred acre property that includes every luxury imaginable. You'd have a world-class spa and restaurant, horseback riding, trout fishing, hiking trails into the national forest, and most important of all, absolute anonymity. No one would know you were there. You could stay forever, if you wanted. Just drop out and live in one of their casitas."

Lacy seemed interested. "Really? Can you take me there...or maybe draw me a map?"

"Not a problem," Fernando said. "You just follow the Paseo to Bishop's Lodge Road and drive about five miles toward Tesuque. You'll see it off to your right. You can't miss it."

They drove in silence the rest of the way to the BMW dealership. Fernando had nothing left to say.

When he passed Bobcat Bite approaching the outskirts of Santa Fe, Fernando decided to take the fastest route possible in order to get free of Lacy. He turned onto I-25 and drove south to the Cerrillos Road exit.

From there it was a straight shot north to Camino Entrada.

Fernando turned left onto Camino Entrada and right into the parking lot of Santa Fe BMW, a large building that included two showrooms, one for cars and one for motorcycles. The glass sides of both showrooms displayed the intense colors of the flashy, elegant vehicles. Several used BMWs were parked in the lot surrounding the building.

Fernando pulled up in front of the auto side of the showroom, impressed by the bright blues and reds of the cars he saw through the bank of windows. Looked glitzy and expensive. Too damn expensive for his blood. He'd never owned anything other than Fords, Plymouths, and now a Jeep Cherokee, which was a present from Estelle after his old Plymouth took a few bullets in the Jimmy Mackey case.

A dapper middle-aged man walked out of the showroom to greet them, dressed in a suit and bow-tie. Fernando stifled a laugh. You didn't see many bow-ties around Santa Fe. Bolo ties, yes. Bow ties, no.

"Welcome to Santa Fe BMW," the man said cheerfully, clearly a salesman. "Can I help you?"

Climbing out of the Cherokee, Fernando ignored bow-tie man.

"Are you trading in your Cherokee?" the dapper man asked Fernando, with a worried look on his face. "Good to trade in while it's fairly new, because Jeeps don't hold their value."

Fernando pointed at Lacy, who was just getting out of the Cherokee. "No, I'm with him. He wants to buy a car."

Lacy strutted over to the showroom and held out his hand. "Jack Lacy. What models do you have on the lot?"

Now the salesman smiled broadly. "You're in luck. We have several models on hand and more coming next week. Three new Four-Forties arrived yesterday. Let me show you our selection."

Lacy didn't move. He shook his head. "I'm familiar. I have a BMW at home. I need one now, here. I don't care what color it is, just as long as it's a coupe. I don't want a sedan. Understand?"

The salesman clapped his hands. "Good. I think we have two Four-Forty coupes, one electric and one gasoline."

"I'll take the gasoline version," Lacy said. "I can give you a credit card or write you a check, whichever you prefer."

Taken aback, the salesman said, "Oh, well, okay then. We'll start the paperwork immediately."

Lacy walked around to the rear of the Cherokee and removed his suitcase and gun case. He carried them up to the showroom and placed them on the sidewalk. "Let's do it. I don't have all day."

The salesman glanced at Lacy's gun case. "Ah, I see you're a hunter."

Lacy smiled. "You might say that," he said.

"Deer or elk?" the salesman asked.

"Bigger game," Lacy said and followed the salesman inside.

Finally Fernando was free to escape. He walked softly back to the Cherokee, expecting to hear Lacy's voice at any moment. He didn't.

Fernando climbed into the driver's seat and fired up the big engine. Without looking back, he pulled out quickly on Camino Entrada and turned onto Cerrillos Road. Free at last. He thought.

16

Next morning Fernando celebrated his new freedom by staying home and working in their yard. When he got bored with that he sat down in his study with his laptop and deleted files relating to his business as a private investigator, now that he had officially retired. By Noon he was bored out of his mind. He absolutely had to get out of the house, so he jumped in the Cherokee and drove around the Paseo to Canyon Road and up to his former office. He planned to return the key to his office and take Ruby to lunch at El Farol to celebrate the occasion.

He pulled up to the twin posts where his private eye sign had once hung and set the brake. In the rearview mirror he spotted another vehicle pulling in right behind the Cherokee, effectively blocking him in place. He scrambled out of his seat when he recognized the vehicle–the black Toyota Sequoia that had been making his life miserable. Slamming his car door, he turned to find himself surrounded by the two big gorillas he'd seen with Silva Archivada, both dressed in athletic running suits. One stuck a pistol in his back and the other stuck a pistol in his face. He couldn't move. They had him trapped.

"Get in, Lopez," the bigger of the two gorillas said, the one with the Glock poking against his forehead. The big man pointed to the Sequoia. "Silva wants to talk to you. Now!"

"No thanks, I haven't had lunch yet," Fernando said flippantly. "I'm on my way to El Farol with my friend Ruby. Care to join us? We can walk-it's just down the street."

"Teach him some manners, Mark," the smaller of the two said.

"Don't teach him some manners, Mark," Fernando countered "Let's keep this friendly."

"Go on," Mark said, pushing Fernando toward the Sequoia.

The small gorilla frisked Fernando and then pushed him through the open car door into the rear seat of the Sequoia. Then he climbed into the front passenger's seat and waited for Mark to get behind the wheel.

"Don't try anything funny," Mark said. "Silva just wants to have a conversation. We'll bring you back here when he's done with you."

Fernando couldn't hold his tongue. "When he's done with me? That doesn't sound like much fun."

"Unless you keep smarting off...in which case Silva might get other ideas," the small gorilla said.

This time Fernando kept his mouth shut, resigned. He'd left his Smith & Wesson locked in the glove compartment of the Cherokee. Probably better. No way he could have shot his way out of this mess.

Mark backed up the Sequoia and then shot out of the parking lot up Canyon Road, heading toward the mountains. They entered Upper Canyon Road, the adobes older and duller here, not all glitzed up like the million dollar shops and galleries on lower Canyon Road. Minutes later they approached the old Forest Service building at the end of the road. Achivada's black Range Rover was parked out front of the two-story A-frame, constructed of Ponderosa pine logs.

Mark parked in the center of the spacious parking lot. Fernando had no idea why he parked so far away from the door. Was he expecting another shoot-out like the one Manny was wounded in?

The three of them sat in the car in silence. Fernando began to wonder why they weren't getting out of the Sequoia. Instead, both Mark and the other gorilla stared at the A-frame, waiting for Archivada to come out. Several minutes later the front door of the A-frame opened and Archivada stepped out accompanied by a muscle-bound man wearing a western hat and carrying an automatic rifle. From the distance it looked like an AR-15.

Archivada and his companion walked slowly, nonchalantly across the dirt parking lot to the Sequoia. Taking their sweet time. When they approached, both Mark and the other gorilla climbed out of the Sequoia to meet them. Fernando did the same without being manhandled.

"So we meet again, Mister Lopez," Archivada snapped at Fernando, terse and short.

Fernando flashed a fake smile. "Aren't you going to invite me in?"

The small gorilla jabbed Fernando in the back with his pistol. And then again, for emphasis.

"Owww, take it easy, that's my kidney," Fernando said. "I'm a senior citizen, handle me with care."

"Elijah, no," Archivada said, motioning for his man to step back away from Fernando.

"So what do you want, Archivada?" Fernando asked point blank. "I still haven't had my lunch, as I was telling your two goons here."

Archivada gave Elijah the Evil Eye, warning him to keep his hands off Fernando. Then he turned to Fernando and said, "As I'm sure you know, Jack Lacy has not returned the advance he was given to do a job that he did not do, which means he is in fact stealing from our mutual employer. That is not acceptable to our employer. As I mentioned earlier, there will be consequences."

Fernando raised his hands. "I have nothing to do with Jack Lacy. He means nothing to me."

Archivada shook his head sadly. "That is hard to believe. You see, we saw you leave La Fonda yesterday morning with Lacy and that big cop, his friend. You were also seen with Lacy again yesterday afternoon...in your car. So we come to you in peace to ask where we can find Lacy. Our mutual employer demands that he pay back the money he took, or he must pay with his life."

"Wait a second," Fernando said, trying to change the subject. "Why do you keep saying mutual employer? Why don't you just say the name of the big oil bloodsucker that's paying you?"

Archivada frowned. "You know I can't do that. Anyway, that is beside the point. Where did you take Lacy? He was in your car yesterday, yes? We saw you on Cerrillos Road."

Fernando shrugged. "Yeah, I gave Lacy a ride to town when he refused to live out in Antonio's cabin in the Pecos. I dropped him off at Santa Fe BMW out on Cerrillos Road yesterday afternoon."

Archivada looked skeptical. "Santa Fe BMW?"

"Yeah, he wanted to buy a BMW, so I took him to the dealer on Camino Entrada and dropped him off," Fernando said. "Look, if you don't believe me, you can drive out there right now and ask the people in sales or bookkeeping. A funny looking guy wearing a bow tie came out to help Lacy. I dropped Lacy and his suitcase off and drove away. I didn't go in. That's the last I saw of him and the last I want to see of him. Do you understand?"

Archivada shook his head. "So you are going to stand there and tell me you don't know his location? My friend, I find that hard to believe."

"It's the truth!" Fernando shot back, tired of being pushed around. "Send one of your goons to Santa Fe BMW. They'll tell you I dropped off Lacy and went on my merry way. I want nothing more to do with him. He's been toxic, nothing but trouble since he showed up in town."

Archivada studied Fernando's face for a moment and then nodded. "We will check your story. But if you are not telling the truth, we will come for you again and there will be consequences."

Not that again, Fernando wanted to say but didn't. Instead he wisely held his tongue.

"Take him back," Archivada said to his two gorillas.

Fernando jumped into the rear seat of the Sequoia before Elijah could get near enough to manhandle him. Mark climbed in behind the wheel, joined by a scowling Elijah riding shotgun.

They drove back down Canyon Road to Fernando's now empty office, where Mark pulled up behind the Cherokee. Fernando jumped out of the Sequoia and headed for his office.

Elijah buzzed down his window and said, "You better be telling the truth or we'll be back."

Fernando stopped and turned around. He'd had enough. He stepped up to Elijah's window and spit out, "Yeah, you do that. And come back by yourself. Just you and me, pal!"

With that Fernando turned away and walked to the Cherokee and took his Smith & Wesson out of the glove compartment. He glared at Elijah for a moment and then walked over to Ruby's gallery, the Three Cities of Spain. Furious, hands shaking badly, he stepped up on Ruby's porch and stared at the Sequoia. He stood there and waited until the Sequoia drove off. If they came back, he would shoot both of them. One at a time or both at once. However they came.

Take some deep breaths, Fernando told himself. Calm down. To hell with Archivada and his goons. Lacy too. He wanted nothing more to do with any of them. Why didn't they leave him alone?

After he calmed down, he opened the front door and walked into Ruby's gallery. Once inside he heard Ruby humming somewhere in the rear of the building. Humming a tune he thought he recognized as an old Beatles song. Yep, it sounded like "With a Little Help From My Friends."

"Hey, Fernando," Ruby greeted him, walking into the front room. "I'm heading down to El Farol for lunch, wanna come? I might even call it quits and take the day off. Not much business, so fuck it!"

Ruby's voice cheered him. Lunch at El Farol was the reason he'd left the house this morning, that and returning the key to his old office.

"I'm game," Fernando said, handing the key to his office to Ruby. "Here's my key. I'm officially moved out and officially retired."

Ruby shook her head, looking dubious. "I still think you're making a big mistake, Fernando. What are you gonna do all day? Sit and twiddle your thumbs while you wait for the Grim Reaper?"

Fernando laughed. "I know, I know. I can't stand to sit still. Estelle says I'm OCD."

"No more so than me," Ruby said. "So, here's my proposition. If you change your mind, you can work here in the back room of the gallery. We can just move your furniture over here, whatever you need to set up shop.

I might have to rent your old office to help pay the mortgage that Jimmy left me with. He never bothered to pay his bills, the bastard."

With that, Ruby deposited the key in her desk drawer and locked up the gallery. The two of them walked down Canyon Road to El Farol. The place looked downright empty when they first walked in. Then they spotted Blaine sitting all by his lonesome at their favorite table, under the mural of the flamenco dangers. Still wearing his red Bermuda shorts and fishing vest, Blaine raised a frosty mug of beer and waved them over.

"Jesus, Blaine, don't you ever change out of those red Bermuda shorts and that stupid fishing vest?" Ruby asked, sitting next to him at the table. "How do you run a gallery dressed like that? Getting a good look at you in the light, I just realized how ridiculous you look!"

"Hah! Look who's talking!" Blaine shot back. "You're the one who runs a gallery with clay smeared all over your face and clothes. Half the time you look like you've just smeared war paint all over your face."

Ruby glanced down at her jeans, streaked with dried gray clay. She sighed. "Is someone going to get me a drink, or what?"

The one waitress working the lunch shift was busy at another table, so Fernando took the hint. He walked over to the bar and ordered a margarita for Ruby and a Modelo draft for himself.

"Well, it's been nice, but I must be off," Blaine said when Fernando returned with the drinks. He quaffed the last of his beer. "Ruby, you'll be happy to know that I sold the last of Jimmy's paintings. I'm boxing it up and shipping it out this afternoon. As the beneficiary of his estate, you'll be receiving a nice, fat check in the mail for ten thousand dollars, minus my twenty percent."

"So I'll get eight thousand dollars," Ruby replied. "Whereas I would get ten if I'd sold it in my gallery."

Blaine shook his head. "But Jimmy signed a contract with me. We've been through this a thousand times."

"Hah! Thief!" Ruby shot back as Blaine got up and walked out of La Fonda, still shaking his head.

Fernando started to say something but Ruby cut him off with a wave of her hand. "Don't say anything."

Fernando saluted.

"So, Fernando, what's new with you?" Ruby asked, changing the subject. "Let's talk about your problems."

"It's been a rough two days," Fernando said. "Yesterday I spent the better part of the day running after Antonio and driving Jack Lacy around. Then this morning I was kidnapped by Silva Archivada and the Sinaloa Cartel."

Ruby nearly choked on her margarita. "What? Kidnapped? What are you talking about?"

So Fernando explained what had happened that morning, a longwinded tale of woe that ended with the Sinaloa boys dumping him off here so he could turn in his office key. "The irony is that I don't give a damn about either Jack Lacy or Silva Archivada. Now I find myself caught in the middle of their war."

"Caught between two assassins," Ruby said. "That's quite an accomplishment, even for you. How in the hell did you manage that? I mean, come on, you keep saying you're retired!"

"I am retired. That's what I've been telling everyone, but they won't listen. They won't leave me alone."

"Hah!" Ruby said, as the waitress came over with menus. "Sounds like you need to tell yourself. Just say no."

88   Santa Fe Assassin

17

Fernando awoke determined to stay away from his former office today. He lay awake pondering his predicament. The only way he would ever break his dependency on his morning routine was to avoid Canyon Road altogether. He figured trouble would have a more difficult time finding him if he stayed close to home. That meant he had to find something to do in order to keep his mind busy so that he didn't go to the dark place. He'd spent too much time in the dark place already, hounded by guilt and regret over all the things he should have done but didn't, as well as all the things he should have done differently. No thanks.

After lunch yesterday at El Farol, he'd spent a good part of the afternoon in his study making a list of what he might do in his retirement. Estelle added a few suggestions after she came home from work, including repairs she wanted him to do on their house. First, she wanted him to fix their leaking kitchen faucet, and then she wanted him to sand and paint the outside of their windowsills, where the paint had cracked over the years thanks to the intense New Mexico sun. Fernando hated making repairs, so he put both tasks at the bottom of his list.

Estelle also suggested he take on some volunteer work, as she had done with her church nonprofit. She suggested he volunteer as a coach in the Police Athletic League, where he could coach young people playing baseball during the summer and basketball during the winter. The problem with that was that he knew very little about either sport. Unlike most men, Fernando never really cared much for sports, which he found a waste of time and energy.

Instead, he thought he might volunteer for the Big Brother Program, where he would mentor troubled young people, most likely boys, who needed a steady hand in their lives. That kind of role suited him much better. Since he'd spent his entire working life in law enforcement, he could give them good advice about how to avoid falling into the wheels of the juvenile judicial system, a one-way ticket to prison later in life. That he felt qualified to do.

A hobby might be good, if he had one. He supposed he could find his old Nikon camera and take up photography. He used to enjoy taking photos of his two daughters when they were young. Probably just needed a new battery and a good cleaning. Then he remembered the camera on his cell phone, which he could also use. These days cell phone cameras seemed about as good as most DSLR cameras. What to do with the photos was the problem. Print them? Frame them? Post them online? He didn't have any online social media accounts, but Estelle said she could show him how to join and post photos on Facebook, which would allow him to keep in closer contact with his daughters, since both of them posted frequently on Facebook.

Tired of ruminating, Fernando climbed out of bed and dressed quickly. He remembered Estelle saying something about making them a ham and cheese omelet this morning when he was still half asleep. Sometimes she left food on the stove for him before she left for work. So he walked to the kitchen and sure enough found the remains of a ham and cheese omelet, now cold on the stove. On the other hand Estelle had not left him any coffee this morning, so he made himself a cup in his Keurig. Then he heated the omelet in their microwave until it was warm enough for him to gobble down. When he finished eating, he helped himself to a second cup of coffee and went outside to the patio to greet the morning.

The leaves of the cottonwood trees along the arroyo were beginning to turn yellow. A gentle breeze stirred the leaves, making them glisten yellow in the sunlight that filtered through the trees. He loved living in Santa Fe this time of year, always a riot of color. Soon the fragrant aroma of piñon smoke would be wafting up out of the chimneys on Acequia Madre and Canyon Road. The smell of piñon always made him feel warm and cozy and happy to be living on Acequia Madre Street in Santa Fe, the so-called City Different.

Eventually Fernando got bored with his daydreaming, so he walked to his Cherokee and brought in the one box he'd saved from the mess Sinaloa had left at his office. He carried the box into his study and placed it on his desk. The business records, which he would need for tax purposes, he placed in his office file cabinet. The case files and other material he'd collected from various investigations and kept for reasons that escaped him at the moment he left in the box. Then he sealed the box with packing tape and carried it to his garage, placing it on the makeshift shelves in the rear of the garage that collected all their miscellaneous crap, all the odds and ends they didn't know what to do with. Every time he looked at the shelves he was tempted to throw away the whole damn lot.

When finished, he closed the garage door and headed back to the house. Halfway to the patio he heard a vehicle turning into his driveway. He stopped to check his watch. Why was Estelle coming home so early? But when he turned around he saw Antonio's Wrangler, not Estelle's Camry. Antonio parked near the garage and climbed out of his Jeep waving at Fernando.

Fernando's spirits sank. What now? Somehow his plan had gone awry. He might have stayed away from his office today, but his office had come looking for him and was about to bite him in the ass once again. He wanted nothing more to do with Jack Lacy and Silva Archivada. He'd begun to resent Antonio for dragging him into this mess, which from the look on Antonio's face, was about to take a turn for the worse. Could it get any worse?

Fernando raised his hands. "No more! I sent Lacy to Bishop's Lodge. I'm done with him. Understand?"

"Okay, but wait'll you hear what happened," Antonio said, ignoring Fernando as he came closer.

It occurred to Fernando that he might never hear the end of the Jack Lacy/Silva Archivada saga. Ever.

Antonio shook his head. "I got a call from Stan Corkin, the manager of Bishop's Lodge. He said Jack went and locked himself in his casita and won't let anybody in, housekeeping or anyone else. Apparently Jack's been unfriendly and downright threatening to some of the other guests. Corkin called me because Jack listed me as the next of kin to call in an emergency. Corkin wants me to come talk to Jack and try to get him to change his behavior."

Fernando opened his arms, half begging. "Why doesn't Corkin just ask Lacy to leave?"

"Well, because Jack's paid for an entire month," Antonio said. "And, I suppose, because Jack spends a lot of money."

Fernando kicked at some loose gravel on the driveway. He didn't need to ask, but he asked anyway. "So why are you here? Let me guess. You want me to come along, right?"

Antonio nodded. "Yeah, I could use back up, you know how Jack gets. Plus I could use help if Corkin tries to evict Jack. A go-between. You're good at talking people down, I'm not."

Fernando sighed. "Jesus Christ, Antonio! Yesterday I was kidnapped by two Sinaloa goons. They took me to Archivada, who wanted to know where Lacy was hiding. I told him I didn't know and didn't care. Now if I go with you, they'll find out I'm lying. And they will find out because they watch our every move, believe me. They're probably trailing you right now."

Antonio looked around, up and down Acequia Madre Street, but said nothing in response.

"Did you hear me?" Fernando asked, exasperated.

Antonio remained silent, staring at Fernando.

"Oh shit! Goddamnit to hell!" Fernando said. He turned and walked into his house and went directly to his study, where he kept his Smith & Wesson during the night. He strapped on the holster and then locked the house and followed Antonio to the big man's Wrangler.

"I owe you one, my friend," Antonio said as he climbed into the Wrangler. Fernando followed.

"Let's just say we're even now," Fernando replied. "A fresh start. No debts to pay."

Antonio took the familiar route, the Paseo to Bishop's Lodge Road. Cruising down the long hill to Tesuque, Antonio said, "The thing is, I don't know where else to take him. Bishop's Lodge seems like the ideal place. It's out of the city, lots of privacy, and with all the luxuries he says he needs. He'll never find a better place around Santa Fe."

"Did the manager say anything about ghosts, that Lacy was complaining about ghosts?"

Antonio shook his head. "No. Why? Are there supposed to be ghosts at Bishop's Lodge?"

"I have no idea," Fernando said. "The bishop, maybe. I'm just asking because he made such a big deal about ghosts at La Fonda."

"Corkin just said Jack was paranoid and intimidating the other guests," Antonio added.

Fernando frowned as Antonio turned into the long driveway of Bishop's Lodge Resort. "Do you know where you're going? The layout of this place can be very confusing."

"Yeah, I think. Corkin gave me directions," Antonio said. "He told me to turn left on the outer loop and drive up to the Cottonwood Casita on the northwest corner of the property."

Fernando smiled but said nothing. He was familiar with Cottonwood Casita. That's where Belle Longstreet stayed when she conspired to have her husband murdered back during what became known as his Painted Skull Ranch case. A palatial casita made for someone like Jack Lacy's taste. So why couldn't Lacy be happy living in a place like that, which was exactly what he said he wanted? It made no sense, unless Lacy was certifiably crazy.

Come to think of it, Belle and Jack Lacy had a lot in common. A black widow and a professional assassin: that would be quite a match if they ever got together. Who would eliminate whom?

As Antonio turned onto the outer loop, they had spectacular views of the Santa Fe National Forest on their left, the foothills rising like the humps of green buffalo climbing into the sky. On their right Bishop's Lodge spread out before them: Swimming pools, tennis courts, fitness centers, restaurants, riding stables, and every other luxury that the overclass expected and demanded. Old Archbishop Lamy would turn over in his grave if he could see his simple lodge and chapel now. No doubt about it, the money-changers had not only entered the temple, they'd bought the damn thing and turned it into Disneyland.

Up ahead Antonio pointed to the Cottonwood Casita, a faux adobe that looked newly painted. He pulled up behind a blue BMW, the car Lacy purchased at Santa Fe BMW. The two of them climbed out of the Wrangler and walked through an elaborate flower and cactus garden up to the front veranda. Antonio stopped before knocking on the front door and motioned with his head toward two men standing beside a nearby casita. The two men seemed to be watching them. One wore a blue suit and tie, most likely the manager. The other wore khaki clothing with a can of mace on his belt, most likely a security guard. Were they watching Lacy?

Not wanting to get shot if Lacy were stark raving mad, Fernando stood back a ways while Antonio knocked on the door, lightly.

"Who is it?" Lacy yelled angrily from inside.

"Jack, it's me, Tony," Antonio replied.

Moments later the door flew open and Lacy appeared. As usual, he wore all black clothing and his open carry holster. He motioned for them to enter. When they did, Lacy stuck his head out of the door and stared at the two men watching the casita for several long, uncomfortable seconds.

Suddenly Lacy cursed at the two men and slammed the door closed. "You see? They're watching me!"

Fernando ignored Lacy for the moment and studied the exquisitely furnished casita. He remembered it well: Southwestern décor throughout, everything from Native American patterned upholstery on the furniture to kiva fireplaces in the corners and vigas on the ceilings. Navajo rugs and Georgia O'Keeffe inspired paintings hung on the walls, everything new and shiny and inviting. The kind of place that could almost make you happy for spending a thousand or two a night for a bed and a place to sleep. He saw a full kitchen and multiple bedrooms off the front sitting room. In the sitting room a full bar occupied most of one wall. Next to the bar a door opened onto an enclosed patio complete with wrought iron furniture and brightly colored umbrellas. The works. For those who could afford it.

"Like being in a fishbowl," Lacy continued, taking a seat on an overstuffed sofa. "They won't leave me alone, they're always spying on me."

"Yeah, well, the manager called me today," Antonio said, not bothering to take a seat. "He said you wouldn't let them enter your room and that you were intimidating the other guests, threatening them or something like that."

"I need my privacy!" Lacy snapped. "I don't want any of them coming into my room."

"It's probably only housekeeping bringing towels," Fernando added, trying to help calm Lacy. Who else would want to get near the crazy sonofabitch? No one in his right mind.

"I don't care who it is. I don't want them in my room."

"What about intimidating the guests?" Antonio asked. "That's what he was most concerned with. He said you threatened to kill one of the guests."

"Hah!" Lacy laughed. "His wife was staring at me, so I stared back at her. Her husband took offense and told me to stop. I told him to leave me alone or I would kill him."

"Yeah, that'll do it," Fernando said, not intending the comment to be humorous or even sarcastic.

Antonio shook his head and gave Fernando the Evil Eye.

"Bunch of parasites!" Lacy replied. "Pissants and parasites. Every one of these fuckers was born with a silver spoon in his mouth." He turned to Antonio. "I can't believe we fought and died for these people!"

Antonio remained silent. A deeply troubled look came over his face.

"Well, that may be true, Jack, but what difference does it make really?" Fernando asked, breaking the silence, trying to help Antonio. He sat down on an overstuffed chair facing Lacy. "Just remember, this is the perfect place for you to drop out of the public view and become anonymous. All you have to do is keep quiet and ignore the other guests. You have everything you need here–good restaurants, good recreational facilities, good hiking trails. What else do you need? The intruders are probably just housekeeping coming to your door. All they want is to keep your casita clean and give you clean linen. If it bothers you so much, just put your trash and dirty linen on the porch and tell housekeeping to take the trash and place clean towels on the porch. No big deal. Just relax, man–be calm, cool, and collected. You don't have to be outright friendly, but at least be amenable. And don't let anyone get under your skin. Who cares what they think? Fuck'em!"

After an awkward silence, Antonio and Lacy both broke out laughing.

"Damn, Fernando, you sound like a therapist," Antonio said finally. "A damn shrink."

Fernando smiled. "I've been called worse."

Lacy clucked his tongue. "All right. I'll try to cool it. I just don't want anyone spying on me. If they leave me alone, I should be fine. So if the manager calls you again, tell him I don't want anyone coming inside. They can deliver stuff on the porch, just like you said. Okay?"

"I'll tell the manager," Antonio replied, sounding relieved.

"You do that...and make sure he understands," Lacy said.

Antonio's face brightened. "Listen, I know how much you like to hike. How about we go on a long hike tomorrow morning, just the two of us. We could start on the Mesa trail right here. That hooks up with the Little Tesuque Creek Trail. Round trip it's about a four-mile hike. We could come back here and chow down a big meal? What do you say?"

Lacy cracked a smile. "Hell yes! And let's get drunk! We'll get drunk first and then chow down. Be like old times!"

"Deal," Antonio said. "I'll talk to the manager on the way out. We saw him lurking in the shadows when we drove up."

Lacy saluted as they walked to the door, seeming more relaxed than when they arrived. Except as soon as they stepped outside Lacy slammed the door closed behind them and locked it.

Fernando followed Antonio outside. They found the manager and the security guard still watching the Cottonwood Casita.

Antonio went to talk with the manager, who opened his arms wide as if asking what the hell? "What's his problem?" the manager asked. "Should I call the authorities or what?"

"No, he just wants his privacy," Antonio replied. "Don't call the police, that would send him over the edge."

Antonio went on to explain what they'd worked out with Lacy. That housekeeping should leave towels and clean linen on the porch from now on. And that Lacy, in turn, would leave his dirty linen and trash on the porch for housekeeping to pick up.

Meanwhile, Fernando moseyed up to the security guard, who had gone to sit on the side of a fountain between the two casitas. A short beefy young man, he looked disinterested, as though he would rather be elsewhere. Who could blame him? He ignored Fernando at first, but then looked up at him when it became apparent that Fernando wanted to talk. "Yeah?" he asked simply in a tired, half-hearted voice.

Fernando nodded and tried to look concerned. He glanced back at the Cottonwood Casita and then turned to the guard, unable to control himself. "I'd keep my distance, if I were you," Fernando said. "Lacy just arrived from Eastern Europe. Rumor has it he's a cannibal."

The guard's eyes widened. "What?"

"That's what we hear," Fernando said. "He has a big, twenty-four quart stock pot on his stove. You figure it out."

Now the guard looked worried. He opened his mouth to speak but nothing came out.

"Okay, you're forewarned," Fernando said and wandered off, making his way around the Cottonwood Casita to Antonio's Wrangler.

Antonio joined Fernando a few minutes later, all smiles. Looked like Antonio had secured a stay of execution for Lacy.

"Yep, the manager's okay with the plan," Antonio said. "He's going to speak with housekeeping and tell them not to enter the casita, to leave everything on the porch. Let's get out of here fast, before he changes his mind."

Fernando nodded. "No need to worry. They won't bother Lacy again."

Antonio glanced at Fernando with a quizzical expression on his face.

18

After Antonio dropped him off at his home on Acequia Madre, Fernando decompressed. He just wanted to be alone, away from people and their problems. Quiet time, that's what he needed. So he went into his study and pulled down all the shades on his windows. Leaving the lights turned off, he sat at his desk with his eyes closed for several minutes. He felt his pulse slow and his blood pressure drop as he began to relax. He'd never tried to meditate for real, but as he relaxed he understood how meditation could benefit the weary. Clear the mind. Recharge the body.

Fortunately, the sound of human voices outside brought him out of his reveries and saved him from possibly going to the Dark Place, which is where he usually ended up when he got lost in his own thoughts. The voices got louder as they approached the kitchen door. He recognized them: Ruby and Manny, arguing about something. Fernando had no idea what they were doing at his house.

One or both of them started pounding on the kitchen door. Bang, bang, bang. Sounded like the door was coming apart. "Fernando, I know you're in there," Ruby yelled. "You can't hide from me. We had to come all the way over here to have you settle an argument. I don't like having to come all the way over here!"

"Go away! I'm not home!" Fernando shouted.

Suddenly the door opened and Ruby burst into the kitchen like a tornado. She stomped on down the hallway to Fernando's study.

Fernando laughed. "Ruby, you're a force of nature. Make yourself at home, why don't you."

"Is that an insult?" Ruby asked, looking around the study. "What's wrong with you? Why are you sitting in the dark?"

Fernando threw open his arms. "Just looking for some peace and quiet. What's your problem now? Why are you all worked up...again?"

"He's my problem," Ruby responded, pointing to Manny, who crouched back against the door of the study as if trying to escape Ruby's

JAMES C. WILSON 97

tongue. "I want whoever killed my brother-in-law arrested and charged with the murder. So Tessa and I can file a lawsuit for compensation. She's all alone at their gallery in Abiquiu now. But this lame-ass won't help!"

Manny raised his hand meekly. "That's me, I'm the lame-ass. I keep telling her that this is out of my jurisdiction. The San Juan Country Sheriff would have to arrest the shooter, if they could identify and find him, which they can't. Then it would be up to the San Juan County Attorney in Farmington to file charges. That's how the judicial system works, but she won't believe me."

Fernando responded by again throwing open his arms. He said nothing.

"What do you mean 'if they could identify and find him?'" Ruby shot back. "They have the damn video tape."

"Like I told you, the tape's blurry," Manny pleaded. "They can't identify the shooter."

"What about the shooter's car?" Ruby said, not about to give up so easily. "It's the black Range Rover that's been driving around Santa Fe for weeks now. Are you blind?"

Manny turned to Fernando. "The Range Rover is registered to a Rick Lucero of Chimayo, who's been dead for about ten years. We know it's being used by the Sinaloa Cartel, so we put an APB out yesterday. No one has reported seeing it yet, probably because they've already taken it to a chop shop for a little remodel. It likely has a different license plate or paint job. Maybe both."

"Don't look at me, I'm not involved," Fernando replied. "How many times do I have to tell you guys that I'm retired. At the moment I'm trying to meditate, so could you both leave?"

Ruby flashed him the Evil Eye and then turned to Manny. "Oh for Christ's sake! Andy's murderers are right here in Santa Fe and you're doing absolutely nothing about it."

"I can't do anything about it, Ruby, the murder occurred in San Juan County and they're unable to identify the shooter. They have to make the arrest and bring charges. It's up to them."

Ruby turned to Fernando. "You see what I'm dealing with?"

"Not my problem," Fernando said.

At that Ruby stormed out of the office, with Manny scrambling to get out of her way.

"Jesus that woman is a hothead!" Manny said, taking a deep breath. "What do you think? Did I get through to her?"

Fernando shrugged. "I don't know. Does anyone ever get through to Ruby? What I do know is that the San Juan County Sheriff's Office is not going to solve this crime. They're even more understaffed than Santa Fe County."

"I know, but I can't tell that to Ruby. God knows what she'd do."

"Exactly," Fernando said. "What she doesn't know won't piss her off."

Manny nodded. "So what's the latest on Jack Lacy?" he asked. "Is Antonio still babysitting him?"

Fernando gave him an update. "So as far as I know, Lacy will be staying at Bishop's Lodge for the entire month, maybe longer if he decides to stay in Santa Fe. Unless he gets kicked out. Which is a real possibility given his inability to get along with other people. He's not exactly a people person."

Manny smiled. "Except for eliminating them, I guess. He's apparently damn good at that."

Manny turned and looked behind him to the kitchen door, which Ruby had left wide open. "Okay, I gotta go. Let's keep in touch. I have no idea how all this is going to play out. Ruby hired none other than Raoul Garcia as her attorney. She wants Raoul to file a lawsuit against Sinaloa, but how are you going to sue a cartel?"

"Well, if anyone can do it, Raoul can," Fernando replied.

"And as for Lacy, I can't understand why he wants to stay in Santa Fe anyway," Manny continued. "I mean, he knows the cartel's after him, so why doesn't he just get the hell out of here? Why stay? He's one man against a cartel!"

Fernando sighed. "Yeah, I don't know why anyone does anything anymore. I'm at my wits end."

Manny stared at him. "Whatever," he said and walked out the door to join Ruby, who just then started honking the horn of whatever car they'd taken, her Honda Accord or Manny's cruiser.

19

Next morning Fernando decided to go check on Ruby to make sure she hadn't done something she'd regret. Ruby had the world's worst temper; she was liable to do anything. So after a leisurely breakfast and an hour or so on his patio drinking coffee, Fernando went into his study and grabbed his Smith & Wesson and headed for the kitchen door. Just then his cell phone rang.

Fernando worried, thinking Ruby had done something drastic. But as soon as he answered the phone he realized that he needed to worry about himself, not Ruby. The voice was unmistakable. The last person he wanted to hear from.

"Mister Lopez, you lied to us," Archivada said in his slow, choppy way of speaking. "We checked out Santa Fe BMW and know that you helped Jack Lacy purchase a BMW and that you gave him directions to Bishop's Lodge Resort. So, you see, that means you do know where he is hiding. That means you will pay the price for trying to deceive us. You and the big cop who's helping Jack Lacy will pay the price. There will be consequences."

With that, Archivada clicked off.

Great. What a way to begin the day. He stood frozen at the kitchen door, trying to decide what to do next. Then he remembered Ruby. He was on his way to Ruby's gallery to check on Ruby.

Suddenly paranoid, Fernando stuck his head out of the door and looked around his yard and then the street beyond. Looked clear, so he locked up and climbed into his Cherokee. On Acequia Madre and then the Paseo he kept an eye out for anything that looked like a Sinaloa vehicle. By the time he turned right onto Canyon Road he felt more confident.

He saw Ruby's Honda Accord parked near the porch of her gallery, so he parked on the other side of the lot near where his private eye sign used to be located. Someone had removed the two posts that held up the smashed, discarded sign, which meant there was absolutely no trace left of his business. Nothing inside his office and nothing out front. Like the business had never existed.

Feeling like a ghost, Fernando stepped out of his Cherokee and took a deep breath, trying to relax. Suddenly he heard an engine start just up the street. Moments later a black Toyota Sequoia came screeching down Canyon Road. Then: Pop! Pop! Pop! The sound of gunfire and breaking glass.

Fernando hit the ground hard and struggled to get his Smith & Wesson out of its holster. He glimpsed the black Sequoia moving slowly down the street and two shooters firing out of the front and rear passenger's seats.

Pop! Pop! Pop! Pop!

Fernando managed to squeeze off a couple of rounds. His bullets thudded into the side of the Sequoia, which then took off fast down Canyon Road. Finally he stood up and ran to the street, still firing at the fleeing car. He stopped shooting as soon as he spotted a group of tourists walking up Canyon Road. The last thing he wanted to do was shoot a tourist.

After the Sequoia disappeared around a long curve, Fernando dusted himself off and turned around. That's when he noticed the Cherokee. The Sinaloa gunmen had shattered every window except the left front. Not only that, but bullet holes lined the right side of the Cherokee, two of them perilously close to the engine.

"Fuck!" Fernando cursed, inspecting the damage. The Cherokee would be impossible to drive, at least for the immediate future.

Hearing him curse, Ruby came out of her gallery next door, followed by Paul and June Bryan on the other side of his former office. The Bryans operated Essentia, which sold sex toys and unguents to those who considered sex a sport for which you needed certain gear.

"What was that?" asked June, a tiny waif of a woman with short blue hair who wore a skin-tight leotard. In fact, Fernando had never seen her in anything but a tight leotard.

"The Sinaloa Cartel," Fernando said. "Be careful. They've established a presence in Santa Fe.

"Jesus, look at your Jeep," Paul said, a clean-cut, button-down young man wearing his usual chinos and polo shirt. He pointed to the damaged Cherokee. "Why are they after you?"

Fernando sighed. "Long story. I got between them and someone who crossed them."

After Paul and June went back to Essentia, Fernando turned to Ruby, who hadn't said a word. "See, this is why you have to be careful dealing with the cartel. You can't threaten them or file lawsuits. If you do, this is what happens."

"Maybe I'll ask Blaine to help," Ruby said. "He knows how to use a gun."

"Ruby, these people are murderers!" Fernando nearly shouted.

Ruby nodded, silent again.

"Actually, I came down here to check on you," Fernando said. "You were pretty worked up yesterday. I thought you might have gotten yourself in trouble."

"Nah, I'm fine," Ruby said. "I talked to Raoul after we left your house yesterday. He said to wait until the investigation concludes and see what happens. He said there may be an opportunity for a lawsuit, maybe not, depending on if and how it all plays out in court. Sounded reasonable."

"Good, listen to Raoul," Fernando said. "He's the best."

Ruby motioned toward the wounded Cherokee. "You'll need to call a tow truck for that. Come on into the gallery while you wait."

Fernando followed Ruby into her gallery. He called his Jeep dealer and sent for a tow truck. While he waited, Ruby made them a cup of coffee and told him about Tessa's plans to move to Santa Fe and help out with Ruby's gallery.

Over an hour later Fernando heard the tow truck turn into his parking lot and honk. He went outside to find an old geezer with a white beard standing beside the Cherokee. The old timer wore overalls and an L.A. Dodgers baseball cap pulled down over his forehead.

"Hell of a way to treat a new Cherokee," the old timer said, when he saw Fernando approaching.

"Yes, it is," Fernando said.

"You must have some serious enemies, my friend," the old timer added, shaking his head.

The two of them jawed for a few minutes about serious enemies and how the world had gone to hell. Then the old timer attached a tow and got ready to leave. "You coming with me?" he asked.

"Yeah, I'll need to rent another Jeep while this is in the shop," Fernando said, climbing into the passenger's seat of the truck.

It took forever for the clunky truck to make it all the way out Cerrillos Road to the dealership while towing the damaged Cherokee. The Cherokee scattered broken glass with every bump on the pavement, attracting the stares of a good many drivers along the way.

Then it took forever to get the attention of a service manager and explain what needed to be done.

And then it took forever to fill out the paperwork to secure another vehicle temporarily. No loaners were available, so Fernando ended up renting a bright yellow Wrangler, the only renter left on the lot. It was the ugliest color he'd ever seen and the most embarrassing to drive. Stuck out on the street like a sore thumb. A far cry from the subtle gray-blue color of his Cherokee.

When he pulled into his driveway on Acequia Madre it was well past Happy Hour at El Farol. He didn't bother to stop at El Farol because he wasn't exactly in a happy mood. He saw Estelle sitting on the patio as he parked the garish Wrangler behind her Camry. She did a double-take, at first thinking she had a visitor and then realizing it was Fernando behind the wheel of the strange vehicle. He waved stepping out of the Wrangler.

"What are you doing with that ugly thing?" Estelle asked. "Where's your Cherokee?"

"It's in the shop," Fernando said, walking to the patio.

"Again? I thought you just had it in?" Estelle asked.

"Something came up," Fernando said, not wanting to tell Estelle about the damage to the Cherokee, a present she had given him when he announced he was retiring. Which, given today's events, he was apparently still in the process of doing.

Estelle looked at him suspiciously.

"I'll be right back," Fernando said, going into the house to get a Modelo.

"Don't hurry," Estelle said in a disapproving tone of voice.

One of those days.

20

Three days later Fernando received a call from a service manager at the Jeep dealership. The good news: his Cherokee was ready to be picked up. The bad news: the bill for new windows, body shop work, and miscellaneous parts was a whopping $2,500 after insurance. Not what he wanted to hear now that he was retiring and would be living on a fixed income. But he had no choice, so he drove the bright yellow Wrangler to the dealership and picked up his Cherokee, which looked as good as new. If, that is, you didn't look too closely.

Back home Fernando parked the Cherokee in his garage, not in the driveway as he normally did. He knew the cartel would find out where he lived, if they didn't already know, and he didn't want to tempt the Sinaloa gunmen by parking in full view of traffic on Acequia Madre. What they couldn't see, they couldn't shoot.

Meanwhile, he hadn't heard a thing from Antonio or anyone else about Jack Lacy and his problems with the cartel. He took that as a good sign. Maybe everyone now realized he had nothing to do with Lacy or Sinaloa. He wanted nothing more than to be left alone, free of their troubles. He was retired, more or less. That's what he kept telling everyone, but no one seemed to take him seriously.

He closed the garage door and walked to his patio and into their adobe. Once inside he felt safe. He went into his study and took off his open carry holster. As soon as he put his feet up on his desk and began to relax, he heard a car pull into his driveway. He hoped it was Estelle, coming home early. No such luck. Heavy footsteps on their flagstone patio ended his peace and quiet. He grabbed his Smith & Wesson and waited for the inevitable knock. When it came, he took his Smith & Wesson and walked into the hallway. Then he stopped, trying to decide what to do next. Should he sneak out their side door and flank the visitor, or should he just stay put to see what the visitor intended and if he would identify himself? Maybe if he didn't answer, the intruder would go away. Wishful thinking.

Instead, the door opened anyway and in stepped none other than Jack Lacy, as usual dressed in black from head to foot, from the black beret on his head to the heavy black boots on his feet. Caught in the light of the kitchen doorway, he looked like a goddamn spectre.

Fernando lowered his pistol.

"The door wasn't locked," Lacy said, tentatively. He stood in the doorway gawking at Fernando.

Fernando frowned. "What do you want, Lacy?"

The tall, gangly Lacy walked stiffly over to the kitchen table and eased himself into one of the chairs. "We have a problem."

That was the last thing Fernando wanted to hear. "No, I keep telling you people that I have nothing to do with your problems. Whatever it is, you deal with it. Leave me alone!"

Lacy shook his head sadly. "Believe me, I wish I could, but it's Tony. He's missing."

"What do you mean, missing?" Fernando asked, now paying attention. He sat down at the kitchen table across from Lacy.

"I shouldn't have come to Santa Fe," Lacy said. "I shouldn't have dragged him into my problems. I blame myself."

"But what about Antonio?" Fernando asked again, starting to worry. "What's happened?"

"He's missing," Lacy repeated. "He doesn't answer his phone. I went out to his cabin in the Pecos to check on him yesterday. His Wrangler was there, and his cell phone was inside on the kitchen table, but he was gone. I waited all afternoon, but he never returned. I'm worried that something's happened."

Fernando didn't know what exactly to make of this. He could never remember seeing Antonio without his cell phone. It wasn't like Antonio to just walk away and leave his phone and his Jeep, unless he walked into the national forest to hike or fish. Except that would be a long walk from his cabin. Still, it was possible, especially if Antonio wanted to go off grid for a while. And he wouldn't get any reception in the Pecos Wilderness, so why take his phone?

"So what do you want me to do about it?" Fernando asked finally, realizing after the fact that he hadn't sounded very friendly.

Lacy stared at Fernando. "You don't like me, do you?"

"Not much," Fernando said, without hesitation. "Why would I? You're an assassin, a killer. I've spent my whole adult life in law enforcement trying to stop people from killing other people."

"Like I said before, it's my profession," Lacy said. "Something I was trained to do in Iraq. I'm good at it, and I can make a living doing it.

What's the difference, here or Iraq? I'm eliminating those who certain people want eliminated."

"Dee Highland?" Fernando shot back.

Lacy shrugged.

"At least in Iraq you killed for some cause, even though the cause might have been a mistake. At least it wasn't for money."

"Give me a break," Lacy said. "Weapons of mass destruction? The Domino Theory? The causes are all bullshit. Nobody over there gives a damn about the cause. It just comes down to people getting trained and paid to kill others."

Fernando did not respond.

"I thought I should tell you, but if you're not interested in helping," Lacy said, starting to get up.

Fernando sighed. "I am interested. Antonio's my best friend."

Lacy sat back down and stared at Fernando.

"Okay, I'll ask around, see what I can find out," Fernando said. "I might even go out to Pecos to check the cabin again. I don't know, maybe he went fishing or camping in the national forest. He does that sometimes when he needs to get away for one reason or another."

Lacy nodded. "Maybe. I don't know. I'm worried about Sinaloa. I shouldn't have gotten him involved."

"Well, let's don't get ahead of ourselves," Fernando said. "Wait until I have a chance to look around."

"Okay, but keep me posted. Whatever you find out, call me right away. Day or night, I don't care. I'm awake most of the night. I hardly sleep anymore."

"Write down your cell phone number then," Fernando said, passing Lacy a note pad he and Estelle used for shopping lists.

Lacy wrote down his number and passed the pad back to Fernando. He nodded and stood up, walking slowly to the door. Then he stopped and turned back to Fernando. "If the Sinaloa Cartel is responsible, I'll kill every one of them in Santa Fe. Every one of them."

Fernando sat silently in his chair watching Lacy walk out the door. Lacy spoke so matter-of-factly, so coldly about killing, that Fernando never doubted him. One of the scariest people Fernando had ever encountered. Seemed capable of doing anything, anything at all.

After Lacy left, Fernando sat brooding at the kitchen table. The more he thought about it, the more unlikely it seemed that Antonio would disappear by choice when his long lost war buddy was in town. Especially a war buddy who needed his help. What to do, that was the question. He decided to pay Manny a visit at the Washington Avenue Station. Maybe there was another explanation for Antonio's disappearance. Manny would know, if anyone would.

So Fernando locked the kitchen door and drove his Cherokee down to the Paseo and over to Marcy Street. He had to park on the damn street like a common tourist now that he'd lost his reserved place in the station parking lot. He found a spot near the coffee shop and plugged the meter, having to scour the floor of the Cherokee for lost dimes and nickels to insert into the meter. Then he walked down to Washington Avenue and over to the familiar building where he'd worked for over thirty years, the last ten or so as chief detective.

Inside he found his old friend Linda at the front counter, sitting behind a vase of roses. "What's the occasion?" Fernando asked.

"Today's my last day," Linda said. "I'm retiring. I decided to follow your lead. Now I can sit at home twiddling my thumbs all day. Or watching reruns of 'Judge Judy' and 'Mash.'"

Fernando laughed. He loved Linda's sense of humor. An old hippie with long gray hair and a wicked sense of humor, she'd moved down to Santa Fe from Taos in the late 1970s after becoming disillusioned with living in the New Buffalo commune. He'd had a brief affair with Linda many years ago, his only indiscretion in the forty years he'd been married to Estelle. They'd broken it off to save their friendship...as well as his marriage.

"No, you'll get used to it," Fernando said. "Just find a hobby, something you like to do."

"How 'bout drinking wine?" Linda replied. "Is that a hobby?"

"Hah! You already do that," Fernando said, laughing. "I mean something new, like paragliding or downhill skiing, something you've always wanted to do but never had the time."

"I'll stick to drinking wine, thank you," Linda said.

Fernando looked around. "Is Manny here? I need to see him."

Linda nodded. "Should be in his office."

Fernando walked down the long hallway to his old office, now Manny's office. Ugly metal furniture, uncomfortable chairs, and one lone window that looked like it hadn't been cleaned this century. Manny was sitting at his desk, which was piled high with paperwork and used Styrofoam cups. He smiled when he saw Fernando. *"Mi casa es su casa,"* he said. "Literally."

"Well, I see you've cleaned up the office," Fernando said, sarcastically.

"Oh yeah, I've kept the office just the way you left it," Manny said. "It's like a museum exhibit, you gotta preserve it. The Detective Fernando Lopez Office. A piece of Santa Fe history."

Fernando laughed. "I feel like a museum piece. Old and creaky."

"No way," Manny said. "You look good...I mean, for your age."

"Thanks. You're too kind."

"So what's up?" Manny asked.

"I'm looking for Antonio," Fernando said. "Have you seen or heard from him lately?"

Manny shook his head. "No. I called and left a message for him yesterday, but he hasn't responded. Why?"

"I got a visit from Jack Lacy this morning," Fernando replied. "He said Antonio was missing. Said he went out to Antonio's cabin in Pecos but didn't find Antonio, only his cell phone and Jeep. He claims Antonio has disappeared."

Manny looked puzzled. "Antonio? That's hard to believe. If anyone can take care of himself, it's Antonio. Maybe he went hiking, or just walked off into the woods on a fishing trip. Something like that. I don't know why anyone would want to, but he loves to fish."

"Yeah, I thought of that," Fernando said, not very convincingly.

"So you're worried," Manny said, a statement, not a question.

Fernando shrugged. "I don't know what to think. I guess I'll go out to the cabin this afternoon and take a look around. Maybe he's returned by now. But I don't know why he wouldn't answer his phone."

"Well, I hope you find him," Manny said, sounding worried.

21

On the drive to Pecos Fernando's worst fears began to get the better of him. What if Antonio had not gone hiking or fishing in the Pecos Wilderness? What if he'd had an accident and lay dying somewhere. Worse yet, what if the Sinaloa Cartel had murdered him and dumped his body somewhere it would never be found? That way Silva Archivada wouldn't have to go through Antonio to get to Lacy. Fernando spun out one grim scenario after another until he was literally covered with sweat by the time he turned into Antonio's driveway.

Seeing Antonio's Wrangler parked beside the cabin buoyed his spirits for a moment, until he remembered the Wrangler had been there when Lacy visited earlier. He pulled up behind the Wrangler and climbed out of his Cherokee. For starters, he circled the Wrangler peering in the windows front and rear. He didn't know exactly what he was looking for but didn't see anything amiss. So he walked to the cabin and knocked on the door. "Antonio?" he called, and knocked on the door again.

Suddenly he heard a cell phone ring inside the cabin. The sound jolted him for a moment. Did that mean Antonio was inside, back from wherever he'd been?

Fernando threw open the unlocked door and stepped inside. There, on the kitchen table, he saw Antonio's cell phone ringing and its screen flashing. He debated whether to answer the call, but the ringing stopped before he could pick up the phone. He checked the number of the caller. Manny's number.

Leaving the door open to provide light, Fernando scoured the cabin. He looked for any sign of a struggle or blood from a serious injury, anything that would explain Antonio's absence. Looked about the same as it always did. Dirty dishes, items of clothing, and blankets cluttering every piece of furniture in the cabin. Antonio was a real slob, after years of living by himself in a primitive cabin. Probably be hard to tell if a struggle had occurred here.

Then he spotted something shiny on the floor over by the cast-iron wood stove. He moved slowly through the clutter, finding two glass TeleDarts on the dirty wooden floor. Empty TeleDarts. Meaning someone had fired a TeleDart tranquilizing gun here recently. On the floor beside the wood stove he also found several drops of what appeared to be dried blood, suggesting the tranquilizing gun was fired inside the cabin. To Fernando's knowledge, Antonio did not possess a tranquilizing gun. And as a self-described recluse, Antonio had very few visitors, if any. Yet someone had to fire the TeleDarts.

Fernando froze, trying to wrap his mind around what he was seeing. Could someone, maybe one of the Sinaloa gorillas, have shot Antonio with an animal tranquilizing gun and then kidnapped him? Or worse, murdered him and then disposed of his body? They would have to put him out cold to kidnap him. Not only huge and strong as an ox, Antonio was a raging beast when angered.

Troubled, Fernando carefully searched the rest of the one-room cabin but found no other signs of a struggle. No overturned furniture or broken glass, nothing that would indicate a struggle had occurred. Finally he gave up and walked back outside, where a dark cloud had moved in from the west, blocking the sun. He felt a chill in the air, reminding him that he was in the Pecos Wilderness, not in sunny Santa Fe. Before leaving, he decided to search the trail behind Antonio's cabin that led into the national forest. He didn't know what he might find on the trail. Hopefully not Antonio's body. He couldn't leave without at least checking it out.

Walking fast now, he climbed a gradual slope into the tall ponderosa pines. He stopped to search every spot along the trail where hikers had stopped to rest, each of the areas littered with plastic water bottles, food wrappers, and assorted trash. No sign of Antonio. When he came to a side trail, he searched the trail for a hundred yards or so and then returned to the main trail.

After about a mile he called it quits and headed back down the trail. He didn't know what he was looking for, but whatever it was, it would be next to impossible to find it on a trail that extended for miles, possibly all the way to the ski basin. Like looking for a needle in a haystack. If Antonio had been kidnapped or murdered, whoever did it would likely take Antonio or his body with them.

Leaving the shade of the ponderosas, Fernando saw a car pulling into Antonio's driveway, a Santa Fe Police cruiser. By the time he reached Antonio's cabin the cruiser was parked next to his Cherokee. Manny stood beside the cruiser, checking his cell phone. When he saw Fernando, the little man pocketed his cell phone and walked over to the cabin.

Manny pointed to the ponderosas on the hill. "Were you looking for Antonio up there?"

"Yeah, but I didn't find any sign of him on the trail," Fernando said. "Come take a look inside the cabin."

Manny followed Fernando into the cabin. "Looks about the same... as messy as ever."

Fernando pointed to the TeleDarts on the floor near the wood stove, which he hadn't touched. "Take a look."

Manny bent down and picked up one of the empty projectiles. "So what do you make of this?"

Fernando shook his head. "Well, considering the drops of dried blood on the floor, either Antonio used a tranquilizer gun on a fairly large animal–maybe the young black bear that kept getting into his trash, or maybe a wandering bobcat. Or maybe, and I think more likely, Archivada and the Sinaloa Cartel used it on Antonio and then kidnapped him. That's what I make of it."

Confused, Manny asked, "but why would the Sinaloa Cartel want to kidnap Antonio?"

"Maybe because they think he's trying to protect Lacy," Fernando said. "To get Antonio out of the way. That's my guess, anyway."

Manny studied the dart. "Hmmm...I don't know what to think. Maybe Antonio was playing around with a tranquilizing gun and shot himself in the foot, something like that."

Fernando wasn't convinced. "I doubt that, Antonio's very careful with his weapons. All that military training."

"Well, one thing's for sure, Antonio wouldn't be that easy to kidnap," Manny said.

"No, he wouldn't," Fernando responded, "unless, of course, they used a tranquilizer gun on him."

Manny nodded. He searched behind the wood stove and then circled the cabin floor looking for other signs of a struggle. Finally he turned and stared at Fernando. "What do you think we should do?"

Fernando shrugged. "Wait until we hear from Antonio, or from whoever kidnapped him, I suppose. Unless you can think of somewhere else he might be. He doesn't have any friends besides the two of us, as far as I know."

"And Jack Lacy," Manny added. "You don't think Lacy could be involved in this, do you?"

"I don't see how," Fernando said. "Why would Lacy want to tranquilize and kidnap Antonio? They're old war buddies. One of the few friends Antonio has."

"Yeah, Antonio's a loner, for sure," Manny mumbled. Then he made his way out of the cabin and looked up at the foothills behind the cabin. He sighed. "Okay, I'll spread the news at the station. Let me know if you hear anything."

After Manny drove off, Fernando lingered at the cabin. He walked around to Antonio's trash receptacle, a 50-gallon drum where Antonio dumped and burned his trash, a common practice in rural areas. He found a myriad of animal tracks surrounding the rusted drum, everything from small raccoon tracks to larger cat and bear tracks. Maybe, just maybe, Antonio had purchased a tranquilizing gun to deal with the animals rummaging through his trash. He kept telling himself that, still wanting to deny the more likely possibility that Antonio had fallen victim to foul play, probably at the hands of the Sinaloa Cartel.

More troubled than ever, he climbed into his Cherokee and headed back to Santa Fe. All he could do now was wait to see if Antonio turned up. That was a problem. Waiting was one thing he did not do well. He needed to keep his mind busy. Otherwise his mind would go to the dark place, where remorse and despair lay in wait to paralyze him. The dreaded dark place.

The waiting game had begun.

22

Next day, tired of waiting, Fernando decided to try to find Antonio by himself. He'd called Antonio every hour on the hour but the big man never answered. So at Noon he decided to go back to the old Forest Service building on Upper Canyon Road, the last place he'd seen Silva Archivada and his gorillas. If Sinaloa had kidnapped Antonio, they may have taken him to the secluded A-frame that bordered the Santa Fe National Forest. At the moment he had no other leads.

Fernando decided to take his Smith & Wesson, just in case things got ugly. After locking the kitchen door, he climbed into his Cherokee and drove down Acequia Madre and around the Paseo to Canyon Road. When it turned into Upper Canyon Road he began looking for the telltale alley to the late Wayne Fontenot's old adobe. He had an idea of how he could observe the old Forest Service building and still remain undetected.

When he saw the alley, he turned sharply to the right and proceeded up a gentle rise to the small adobe where Wayne had lived for the last several decades of his life. A down and out painter, Wayne painted dark, spooky Santa Fe landscapes that rarely sold because most people, tourists and locals alike, found them too depressing to hang on their walls. When Wayne died last year, the other artists on Canyon Road gave him a rowdy, drunken send-off at El Farol.

Fernando's plan was simple. There was a seldom-used hiking trail behind Wayne's adobe that led all the way into the Santa Fe National Forest. The trail curved around behind the old Forest Service building as it climbed into the foothills. From the trail he could scout out the activities at the building below without being seen. If Antonio had been kidnapped, Fernando believed this could be where Silva Archivda was holding him.

Fernando parked his Cherokee behind Wayne's adobe, where it wouldn't be seen from the road. Before leaving he grabbed his binoculars and his open carry holster holding his Smith & Wesson, just in case. Just in case of what he didn't want to think about. Buckled up, he headed up the trail, walking at a steady pace over a long stretch of rocky terrain. Soon the rocky terrain gave way to grassland and scattered piñon and gnarly juniper trees.

When Fernando crested the hill, he got his first glimpse of the two-story log building, an A-frame once owned by the Forest Service and last year sold to Silva Archivada. He stopped when he saw the parking slot in front of the A-frame was empty. Neither of Silva's vehicles, the Range Rover nor the black Sequoia, was in sight. The place looked deserted. On the other hand, one or more of the Sinaloa crowd could be inside holding Antonio prisoner while the others were out. He couldn't leave without finding out.

Eventually the trail took him around behind the A-frame. He found a boulder to hide behind and took out his binoculars. From his perch he could see no activity in or around the A-frame, no sign of anyone. So he scrambled down the hillside, sliding through patches of sage and chamisa, until he reached the bottom. From there he crept quietly up to the rear of the A-frame, looking in the window of a small kitchen. A hallway ran from the kitchen to a spacious front room, empty of furniture. He tried the kitchen door but found it locked. So he took his lock-pick out of his pocket and helped himself.

Fernando opened the door as quietly as possible and stepped inside. He heard nothing, only silence. He left the kitchen door open behind him and tip-toed into the interior of the A-frame. All the rooms on the first floor were empty, so he moved to the stairway leading to the second floor. "Anybody up there?" Fernando called, hearing his voice echo on the walls of the stairway.

No answer.

Taking his Smith & Wesson out of its holster, Fernando started up the stairs. He took one step at a time and then paused to listen. Nothing.

At the top of the stairway he found two rooms, one with a single cot and several suitcases standing against the wall. The other had four air mattresses spread out on the floor. On each mattress was an open sleeping bag and assorted dirty clothes. Duffel bags and plastic bags from Kaune's Market were piled up in one corner of the room. In another corner he found green garbage bags filled with trash, mostly fast-food containers and empty plastic water bottles and beer cans.

Fernando skipped the dormitory and walked into the room with the stacked suitcases. He tried to open the largest of the suitcases but found it locked. When he placed it flat on the floor to try to jimmy it open with his lock pick, he heard something outside. At first he thought it was an airplane flying overhead. Then he realized it was a vehicle coming down the drive to the A-frame.

Don't panic, he told himself. Time to focus. He scurried over to a south-facing window and saw Archivada's Range Rover, now painted a mottled gray, driving into the parking lot in front of the A-frame. One heavy-set man was behind the wheel, another in the passenger's seat. The rear seats looked empty.

No time to waste. He turned and bolted down the stairs. Then he ran down the hallway to the kitchen and out the back door, careful to close the door behind him but not careful enough to lock it again.

Outside, he ran up the hillside into the national forest. When he reached the boulder along the trail, he paused to get his breath. He heard two car doors slam on the other side of the A-frame and then the two men talking, saying something he couldn't make out.

Suddenly he realized he hadn't remembered to lock the kitchen door, nor had he remembered to set the large suitcase upright, like the others in the makeshift bedroom. He'd been careless. The Sinaloa gorillas would notice the change and know an intruder had been in the A-frame.

Cursing, he sprinted down the trail away from the A-frame. He didn't bother to look back. Feeling his age, he had to stop several times to get his breath. By the time he descended the last hill and approached Wayne's old adobe, he was covered in sweat. And exhausted. So he rested against the Cherokee for a few minutes to regain his strength and to plan his next move. He'd seen no sign that Antonio had ever been held captive at the A-frame. Maybe Antonio had gone on a fishing trip, after all. Why not? The big man loved to fish. And, come to think of it, taking off on a fishing trip would be a convenient way to distance himself from Jack Lacy.

Somewhat relieved, Fernando climbed into his Cherokee and drove back down Canyon Road. He decided to stop at Ruby's gallery and catch up. When he pulled into the parking lot he saw Ruby watering a pot of gnarly red geraniums on the porch of her gallery. She waved and motioned for him to come over. He locked the Cherokee and walked across the parking lot to her Three Cities of Spain Gallery. Every time he saw her brightly colored sign he remembered the famous Santa Fe restaurant of the same name, closed now for several decades.

"Got time for a cup of coffee?" Ruby asked, placing her watering can on the side of the porch.

"All the time in the world," Fernando replied. "I'm retired. Or supposed to be retired."

"Hah! You keep saying that but you're always in your office or running around chasing bad guys," Ruby responded. "You're never going to retire!

You're too much like me—you have to keep busy, or you'll go nuts."

Fernando laughed. "So what's new with you?"

Ruby shook her head. "You'll never believe this. It's like a television soap opera. Turns out Andy knocked up one of the wives he screwed up in Abiquiu. The wife's husband knows about Andy and wants Tessa to pay child support. Can you fucking believe that?"

Fernando didn't know what to say, so he said nothing.

"It's a good thing Andy's dead," Ruby said, "or I'd have to shoot the bastard myself."

Fernando followed Ruby into her gallery, where Ruby made two cups of coffee with her coffee maker and served them at the counter in her office. While they sipped their coffees, Ruby gave him an update on Tessa, who had decided to sell her gallery in Abiquiu and move to Santa Fe.

"Yeah, she decided to move in with me," Ruby said, sounding a bit skeptical, which surprised Fernando. "I know it was my idea, and I know she's my sister and all, but I'm starting to have second thoughts. I mean, I haven't lived with anyone since I threw Jimmy out on his ass. You probably haven't noticed, but I'm getting a little cranky and set in my ways. I don't know if I can stand to live with anyone else, even my sister, you know what I mean?"

Fernando laughed, feeling relaxed for the first time all day. Ruby always managed to pick him up, no matter what. He'd never seen Ruby depressed and only once seen her cry: during Wayne Fontenot's memorial at El Farol. She didn't even cry when her ex-husband Jimmy Mackey was murdered in Taos, just got angry at the thugs who killed Jimmy.

"You? Cranky?" Fernando asked. "I don't believe it!"

Ruby eyed him suspiciously. "Are you making fun of me?"

23

Fernando's relaxed mood ended as soon as he stepped outside. His cell phone rang while he walked across the parking lot. He bypassed his Cherokee and headed for the wooden bench out front of Essentia. When he sat down and clicked the accept button, he heard the familiar voice of Santa Fe County Sheriff Jodie Williams:

"Hey, Fernando, Jodie here. There's something going on at the building that burned in Pojoaque, the old Line Camp building that Silva Archivada bought earlier this year. Someone who lives up the road reported lots of comings and goings and what they called suspicious activity. I thought you might want to check it out, since you were so interested earlier."

"What kind of suspicious activity?" Fernando asked.

"I don't know any more than that," Jodie said. "I'm tied up here in Glorieta at the moment but hope to make it out sometime later this afternoon. Talk to you later."

She clicked off before Fernando could get any more information. Now what? He walked back to the parking lot and climbed into his Cherokee. Sitting back in the driver's seat, he reflected on this latest news. Once again the possibility that the Sinaloa Cartel had kidnapped Antonio and was holding him hostage, now at the old Line Camp in Pojoaque, seemed like the most likely explanation for Antonio's absence. That meant he would have to make another road trip to check it out. He cursed, tired of running around looking for Antonio who seemed to have disappeared from the face of the earth. He was plumb out of patience.

Better now than later, he figured. So he fired up the Cherokee and pulled out on Canyon Road. This time he decided to drive right up to the building and ask to see Archivada. Why not? He had a somewhat civil relationship with Archivada. Why not just ask him about Antonio instead of sneaking around trying to spot Antonio on the sly? The cartel either had him or they didn't. If they had him, what did they want to release him unharmed? If they didn't have him, then Fernando could forget about it and get on with his retirement. Once and for all.

He took the paseo around to Highway 84/285, speeding past the Tesuque exit and the Santa Fe Opera. As always he slowed down entering the Pojoaque commercial strip, with the Buffalo Thunder Casino on his right and the blue/green Jemez Mountains straight ahead. He bypassed the turn-off to Los Alamos and followed the curve around to the old Line Camp building.

After Jodie's report of lots of activity around the building, Fernando was surprised to find utter calm as he turned into the parking lot. Desolation might be a better word given the condition of the building, its front blackened by the recent fire and smoke. Part of the roof had buckled, leaving a gaping hole in the front section of the roof open to the elements. Sheets of particle board covered two banks of windows and the opening where the front door had been, on which someone had painted 'KEEP OUT' in huge black letters. Below the letters a sloppy painting of a human skull bled streaks of black paint down the side of the particle board.

The acrid smell of burned wood and melted plastic made him cough when he stepped out of his Cherokee. He covered his nose momentarily until the coughing stopped. There wasn't a person or a vehicle anywhere in front of the building, so he walked around behind the building on a narrow alley intending to check out the small house where he and Jody had talked to Archivada. What he saw puzzled him. Parked between the burned building and the house was an old dented tear-drop trailer attached to an even older Dodge pickup. Originally a matching light blue color, both trailer and pickup had faded from too many years in the sun to a dull gray color, punctuated by large patches of rust along the underside of the carriages. Looked like both belonged in an auto salvage yard.

"Hiya, can I help you?" someone called out from behind the trailer, surprising Fernando.

Fernando jumped, reaching for his Smith & Wesson. "Who's there?" he asked loudly.

"Homer B for Ben Stiles," a disembodied voice said.

Fernando eased around the side of the trailer, right hand on his Smith & Wesson. Then he spotted the speaker, an elderly man wearing a beat-up straw hat sitting behind the trailer in a cheap aluminum lawn chair. The old timer struggled to stand up, thin and emaciated, with a wrinkled face partly covered by a scraggly beard, more white than gray. He looked like someone who lived on the streets, a homeless bum.

"Can I hep you?" Stiles repeated, buttoning the loose straps of his denim overalls, which had fallen down to his waste when he stood. He teetered from one side to the other, as if about to fall over.

"Yeah, I'm here to see Silva Archivada, he's a friend of mine," Fernando said, stretching the truth a bit. He put away his Smith & Wesson. The old timer looked harmless enough. He certainly wasn't armed, unless he had a knife hidden somewhere in those overalls.

"He ain't here," Stiles said. "They all left this mornin'. I don't know when they'll be back. That there fire ruined 'bout everything inside."

"So what are you doing here?" Fernando asked.

"Me? I'm watchin' the place for 'em. Yep, Silva seen me parked across the street in that Buffalo Thunder parkin' lot. He offered me one hundred dollars a week to watch his place here. Even gave me the first hundred. I'm supposed to call him if'n I see anyone suspicious comin' around the place here. I got his number right here in my pocket," Stiles said, patting his shirt pocket. Then he looked Fernando in the eye and asked, "Are you suspicious?"

Fernando frowned. Didn't sound like Archivada would be coming back any time soon. Not if Archivada hired the old man to watch the place. That meant he would have to look for Antonio elsewhere. But where?

"You say yer a friend?" Stiles asked, trying again.

Fernando ignored the question. "Did you see a really big guy with them? He's about six-eight and two hundred eighty pounds, looks something like a professional football player."

Chuckling, Stiles said, "Well now, everyone looks big to me. I done shriveled up over the years. Old age, ya know."

"No one in handcuffs...a prisoner?"

The old timer shook his head. "No sir."

"You don't mine if I look around," Fernando said. It wasn't a question. He passed by the trailer and looked in the window. Inside he saw piles of garbage and empty wine bottles littering the bed and floor. Cheap bottles of what's called 'Bum Wine,' Thunderbird and Night Train mostly. One half-full bottle of Mad Dog sat on a small table. The rot-gut wine, along with the filthy contents of the trailer, almost made him retch.

Fernando walked to the burned-out building and opened the rear door. He was greeted by a burst of foul air, a smell of rancid smoke mixed with what smelled like mold. He saw why when he stepped into the dark room, which before the fire had been Archivada's office. Water damage everywhere, from the ceiling panels to the dry wall to the hard wood floor. What was left of the office furniture lay overturned and waterlogged, casualties of the fire department's efforts to save the building.

They'd succeeded in saving only a burned-out shell that would have to be demolished. He poked around the ruins looking for what he didn't know. Finally he gave up and stumbled outside, gasping for clean air.

"Stinks, don't it?" Stiles said, holding his cell phone. Then he put his phone back in his pocket.

Fernando stared at Stiles. "You just call someone?"

"Yessir, I had to call Silva and tell him 'bout you."

Angry, Fernando went for Stiles but then stopped himself. It wouldn't do any good to manhandle the old man. He was just doing what Silva paid him to do. The old bastard needed money for his wine.

"You ain't gonna shoot me, are you?" Stiles asked, eyeing the Smith & Wesson on Fernando's belt.

"No, I'll let you drink yourself to death," Fernando said, not very kindly.

With that Fernando turned and walked away. He hurried around to the front of the building and climbed into the Cherokee. Spinning out on the highway, he didn't look back.

24

Fernando cursed when he saw the blue BMW parked in front of his garage as soon as he turned into his driveway. *Déjà vu* all over again, as Yogi Berra famously said. No question about it, the car had to be Jack Lacy's BMW, the very same one he'd purchased at Santa Fe BMW. For a split moment Fernando thought of backing up and driving off, maybe go down to the Plaza for a cup of coffee. But he didn't. Apparently this day from hell would continue one way or another. Might as well be here, on his own turf. What did a man have to do to retire in peace?

Not a happy man, Fernando continued on down the drive and parked beside the blue BMW. He sat in his Cherokee for a moment fuming, trying to put on his game face. Suddenly it dawned on him that the BMW was empty. So where was Lacy? He couldn't imagine Lacy being out for a mid-afternoon stroll on picture perfect Acequia Madre Street. More likely he would find Lacy sitting in his living room, after having invited himself in, just as he had done earlier. The man didn't need an invitation. Fernando shook his head, realizing he'd become a cranky, cynical old man. But so what? It went with the territory.

After climbing out of his Cherokee, Fernando looked around to see if he could spot Lacy somewhere nearby, either in his yard or in the cottonwoods at the edge of the property. He didn't see Lacy. No surprise. Just to be sure, he walked carefully up to the BMW and looked in the windows. Maybe the man had fallen asleep in the car or died from a heart attack or whatever. He circled the Beamer but saw no one inside, which meant that Lacy was somewhere on the premises, as he suspected.

Fernando took out his Smith & Wesson to be on the safe side. Who knows what Lacy wanted? The man was a professional assassin. On second thought he put the pistol back in its holster. Why take a chance on riling up Lacy? If Lacy was crazy enough to announce his presence by parking in the open, in full view of everyone, then he had surely come in peace, yes? Better to play it cool.

Even so, Fernando carefully crept up to the house trying to make as little noise as possible. Coming closer, he spotted Jack Lacy sitting in his–Fernando's–favorite spot on their patio bench, making himself right at home. As if he had taken over Fernando's identity.

"I've been waiting for you," Lacy said, interrupting Fernando's thoughts.

"What...what do you want?" Fernando sputtered.

"We need to talk," Lacy said, holding up a lock pick, the exact same one Fernando himself used. "I was waiting for you in your kitchen earlier before I decided to come out here and get some fresh air. I didn't think you'd mind, now that we're friendly."

Since when were they friendly, Fernando wanted to know. But he said nothing. Instead he walked over and sat down in one of the Adirondack chairs facing the bench, his bench. He shook his head, a sign of resignation. Let it happen, come what may. He felt helpless. And doomed.

"I heard from Archivada," Lacy said, again speaking out of the corner of his mouth like a goddamn ventriloquist. "I knew you'd want to know right away, so here I am."

"Here you are," Fernando repeated.

"Take a look, this text just came in a couple of hours ago," Lacy said and held out his phone.

Fernando took the phone and read the text: "If you want to see your friend Antonio alive again, have two hundred fifty thousand dollars in hundred dollar bills delivered to the Forest Service building on Upper Canyon Road tomorrow at Noon. Send Lopez by himself unarmed to deliver the money. He knows where the Forest Service building is located. If Lopez doesn't bring the money at Noon, your friend will be dead within the hour. Silva Archivada."

Fernando did the math, his mind spinning. Ten one-hundred dollar bills would total one thousand dollars. Therefore, it would take two thousand, five hundred one-hundred dollar bills to total two hundred fifty thousand dollars. Where could you get that many one-hundred dollar bills in less than twenty four hours? And why him? Why Fernando?

Then Fernando remembered: this was Antonio, his best friend. That's why he had to help.

"You see, they want you to deliver the money," Lacy said. "They think because Tony's our friend they can get me to return the advance by holding Tony hostage and threatening to kill him."

Fernando threw up his hands in exasperation. "Goddamn it! Why didn't you just settle with them earlier? Give the money back? You're gonna get Antonio killed! For what? For two hundred and fifty thousand dollars? That's small change for you! Why are you so stubborn?"

Lacy stared at him, seemingly uncomprehending.

"And where are you going to get that many one hundred dollar bills so fast?" Fernando asked.

"I'm not," Lacy said, his voice almost a whisper.

"What do you mean?" Fernando asked.

Lacy frowned. "I don't return advances. I told Silva that once. I'm not telling him again."

Fernando bolted up from his chair. "What? If you think I'm going in there without the money, you're fucking crazy!"

Lacy frowned.

"And what about Antonio?" Fernando asked, leaning in so that he was almost in Lacy's face. "Are you just going to leave him there? I thought you were friends, bosom buddies from the Marines."

Lacy waved him off. "Not a problem. I have a plan."

"Of course you do," Fernando said, sighing. Lacy, he realized, always a plan.

25

To Fernando Jack Lacy's plan sounded like a suicide mission. Fernando was supposed to deliver a duffle bag stuffed with newspapers and magazines to the Sinaloa compound at the old Forest Service building and to somehow make sure they brought out Antonio in the parking lot to meet him. Lacy promised to do the rest. Just what the rest entailed, Fernando had no idea. Nor did he have any idea how many men Archivada had with him in the A-frame or much of anything else. Most maddening, he had no idea how he had come to be involved in such a dangerous and impossible plan. That is, he had no idea why he had allowed himself to become involved. He knew it was his own damn fault.

That morning he'd waited until Estelle left for work to prepare the duffle bag. He stopped her on the way out the door and gave her a big hug. Estelle, surprised, asked, "What's gotten into you?"

"Just wanted to hug you, that's all," Fernando said.

Estelle looked at him suspiciously. "O-kay, I'll see you tonight then," she said and hugged him back.

After he heard her Toyota Camry drive off on Acequia Madre, Fernando went into his study and rummaged through the closet looking for the beat-up duffle bag he used on short trips. Then he remembered he'd tossed it in the hall closet after his recent trip to Taos. He went to the hall closet and dusted off the old bag and then stuffed it with old magazines and newspapers. He had no idea how much 2,500 one-hundred dollar bills would weigh, so he had to estimate the appropriate weight. He kept changing his mind, adding more paper and then deciding what he had was too heavy or bulky and removing what he'd just inserted. Finally he gave up, deciding that if all went well none of the Sinaloa gorillas would ever open it anyway. So why worry about it?

According to Archivada's instructions, he was supposed to come unarmed. But he'd be damned if he would walk into a cartel hornet's nest without his Smith & Wesson. So he slipped the pistol into a side pocket on the duffle bag, which would provide easy access. Now the duffle bag felt too heavy, so he removed some of the magazines and added more crunched-up newspapers. Then he realized he would be handing over his pistol when he handed over the duffle bag, so he put back the magazines and went into his study to find a concealed carry holster that fit inside the rear of his pants. Took him a while, because he hadn't used the small holster in years, but he found it on the top shelf of his closet. This would be perfect.

Fernando checked his watch. Nine o'clock, still too early. He had an hour to wait before meeting Lacy on Canyon Road. They'd agreed to meet in the parking lot of his former office.

The longer Fernando waited, the more nervous he became. About nine forty-five he said the hell with waiting. He placed the duffle bag in the rear hatch of his Cherokee and drove to the Paseo and around to Canyon Road. For some reason neither Ruby's gallery nor Essentia was open when he pulled into their parking lot. He sat in the Cherokee thinking about what could go wrong in their plan. Somehow he had to get Archivada to bring Antonio out into the parking lot, where Archivada and his men would be vulnerable. That was the first thing. Then he had to keep the duffle bag away from the gunmen until after the exchange. If the gunmen opened the bag before the exchange, all hell would break loose. Then, finally, he and Antonio had to get clear before or while the gunmen opened the bag. If they didn't, they would get caught in the crossfire. Nasty business.

Lots could go wrong. And in Fernando's experience, anything that could go wrong, would go wrong. That was his rule of thumb.

A few minutes later Lacy's BMW pulled into the parking lot. Lacy climbed out of the BMW and nonchalantly walked over to his Cherokee, knocking on the driver's side window with his knuckles. The man in black looked incredibly relaxed, given the circumstances. Cool, calm, and collected. Nerves of steel. Apparently only ghosts riled the man.

"Okay, did you bring the duffle bag?" Lacy asked, when Fernando lowered his window.

Fernando nodded. "It's in the Cherokee, stuffed with newspapers and magazines like you said."

"Good, now you need to take me to this hiking trail you mentioned, the one that circles behind the building where they're holding Tony," Lacy said. "I need to get set up."

"Yeah," Fernando said, resigned. "It's a fairly long walk from where we park, but you should have plenty of time to get set up."

"Let me get my rifle," Lacy said. He opened the trunk of his BMW and took out his sniper rifle, a SAKO TRG 42 with scope and tripod. He carried the heavy rifle over to Fernando's Cherokee and carefully placed it in the rear hatch. Then he walked back to the trunk of his BMW and buckled on an ammunition belt. "Ready," he said, mostly to himself.

Fernando waited while Lacy climbed into the passenger seat of the Cherokee. Then he backed up and eased out on Canyon Road, nearly running over an unsuspecting tourist with a huge camera. "Sorry," Fernando yelled out the window.

The tourist gave him the finger.

"Do you want me to shoot him?" Lacy asked.

Fernando gave him a dirty look.

"I'm joking, lighten up," Lacy added.

Fernando drove up Canyon Road to Upper Canyon, where he slowed down looking for the alley to Wayne's old adobe. When he spotted the blue house he turned a sharp right into the alley and proceeded up the hill to the now abandoned adobe. As far as he knew Wayne had no heirs, so the dilapidated structure and its surrounding acres in the foothills of the Santa Fe National Forest were in legal limbo.

As before, Fernando parked behind the old adobe so the Cherokee couldn't be seen from the road. Lacy unloaded his sniper rifle and tripod, which he carried by means of a leather strap around his shoulder. He waited for Fernando to lead him to the trail and then followed along behind in silence. They climbed into the foothills, where the trail curved west, back toward Upper Canyon Road. Finally the old Forest Service building came into view, nestled in the canyon below.

Fernando pointed to the A-frame.

"Yeah, I see it," Lacy said. "I need to get a little closer and find just the right angle."

So they continued on until they came to a small clearing where a row of boulders looked over the canyon. From there the A-frame was about seventy-five yards away. Lacy walked to the end of the row sizing up the angle. "I need a diagonal line...not a frontal, and not a side shot," Lacy explained, motioning to the parking lot below. "So I want you to come in on what to you will be the right side of the parking lot, about halfway between the middle of the lot and the right edge. Then I want you to stop about halfway to the door of the A-frame and stay there. Do you understand? That way when they walk toward you I'll have a diagonal shot, okay? This is important for you to remember."

"I understand," Fernando said, irritated at all Lacy's directions.

When he found just the right boulder, Lacy assembled his equipment and scoped out the scene below. Fernando joined him. They saw the Toyota Sequoia parked on the far side of the A-frame, but nobody near the vehicle. Soon they heard a rumble in the distance and then saw a cloud of dust kicking up on the driveway into the parking lot. Moments later Archivada's Range Rover materialized out of the dust, pulling up finally near the front door of the A-frame. Archivada's two gorillas jumped out first, followed by Archivada himself.

"Look, I think that's Antonio in the back seat," Fernando said, pointing to the Range Rover.

While they watched, one of Archivada's gorillas opened the door and grabbed Antonio, dragging him out of the Range Rover. Antonio, whose hands were handcuffed in front of him, pushed the thug away forcibly. The other gorilla poked a pistol in Antonio's back and pushed him toward the A-frame. He continued to push and poke Antonio all the way to the A-frame, where someone opened the door. The two of them disappeared inside.

Archivada lingered in the parking lot, wearing a low-cut khaki shirt with a gold chain dangling from his neck. He checked his wristwatch and then looked around the surrounding hills. Finally he turned and walked into the A-frame.

Meanwhile, Lacy had been watching Archivada through the scope on his sniper rifle. He nodded. "Not going to be a problem," he mumbled to himself.

Fernando shook his head, amazed at Lacy's confidence. Like the guy refused to believe that his plan could backfire, that something could go wrong. Fernando always took the opposite approach. He was usually correct.

Fernando checked his watch. Twenty minutes past eleven. That gave him plenty of time to walk back to his Cherokee and drive up to the A-Frame.

"You remember what to do, right?" Lacy asked.

"I do," Fernando said. "I'm on my way."

With that, Fernando made his way back down the trail to the Cherokee. He took his time. He was in no great hurry to meet up with Archivada, but he had a job to do, so like always he got on with it without overthinking. Thinking too much could incapacitate a man, cripple him. The best way to deal with anxiety was to act.

"Don't think, just act," he said out loud.

As it turned out he timed it perfectly. His watch read five minutes before Noon when he reached his Cherokee. He unlocked the Cherokee and readied the duffle bag on the passenger's seat. Then he made a U-turn and headed down the driveway. Once on Upper Canyon Road he drove slowly, menacingly he hoped, up to the big parking lot in front of the A-frame. He stayed to the right of center, as instructed by Lacy. He stopped about one hundred feet from the door of the A-frame and about the same distance away from the Range Rover.

Once he came to a stop, Fernando scanned the area around the A-frame, looking for potential gunmen hiding on the grounds or in the upper windows of the A-frame. He saw nothing that raised suspicion. So he honked the horn of the Cherokee and held it for several long seconds. Then he climbed out of the vehicle carrying his duffle bag. He stopped a few feet in front of the Cherokee and dropped the duffle bag in the dirt. Then he waited, feeling like a sitting duck. Like a goddamn fool.

Moments later Fernando saw shadows moving inside the front window. Eventually the front door moved slightly and then opened wide. Archivada himself appeared in the door. With his low-cut shirt and the gold chain hanging from his neck, and especially with his black hair slicked back with gel, Archivada looked like an old fashion gangster in mafia movies. Archivada nodded when he saw Fernando standing near the duffle bag. He held the door of the A-frame wide open and said, "Good. Now bring the bag here."

Fernando held his ground. "No. Bring Antonio out first."

Archivada frowned. He looked behind him and then turned back to Fernando. "Bring the bag here and you will have what you want. Your friend is alive and well, just inside the door."

Fernando panicked. He looked around, not knowing what to do. Lacy expected him to bring Archivada and the others outside where they would be vulnerable. Cursing, he blamed himself for not having a backup plan. He knew better. At the moment all he could think to do was call Archivada's bluff.

Desperate, he grabbed the bag and turned around, walking slowly back toward the Cherokee.

"Wait!" Archivada called. "Your friend is here."

Fernando turned around, still holding the duffle bag.

Antonio appeared in the doorway, standing beside Archivada.

"Come get him," Archivada said.

Fernando shook his head and continued walking away, ignoring Archivada.

26

"Okay, wait!" Archivada shouted. He stepped carefully out of the A-frame, looked around, and walked slowly toward Fernando holding what looked like the key to Antonio's handcuffs in his hand. Antonio followed a few steps behind, pushed and shoved along by Archivada's two gorillas. The younger of the two kept poking a pistol in Antonio's side. Antonio snarled at his tormentor, swinging his elbows to push the man and his pistol away from him. For a moment Fernando thought Antonio was about to turn on his tormentor, but the big man controlled himself. Antonio wasn't used to accepting physical abuse.

Finally Archivada stopped about thirty feet away from Fernando. He smiled, full of confidence, as if he'd just won the jackpot.

Fernando stared at Archivada, not moving. Expressionless.

"Give me the duffle," Archivada said.

Suddenly a loud explosion erupted from the hill above: Crack!

Instantly the top of Archivada's head exploded, showering Antonio and the two gorillas with bright red blood. Archivada fell backward, landing in the dust.

Then all hell broke loose. The two gorillas ducked, searching the hills above for the shooter. The one with the pistol fired off a couple of wild rounds that ricocheted off the rocky cliff.

Crack! Crack! came the retort from above.

Dropping his pistol, the younger of the two gunmen grabbed his chest and crumpled to the ground.

Instantly Antonio pushed aside the other gorilla and then grabbed him from behind, pulling his handcuffs tight around the man's neck. Half a foot taller and at least eighty pounds heavier, Antonio lifted the smaller man off his feet, choking him. The man's legs dangled in the air, kicking wildly. Not finished, Antonio jerked the man's head back so violently that Fernando heard the neck snap like a twig. Then Antonio dropped the dying man, who lay twitching in the dust for a few brief seconds before falling still. He didn't move again.

Free of his tormentor, Antonio scrambled over to Archivada and pried open his hands to get the key to the handcuffs. Fumbling with the key, he shouted to Fernando, "Watch out, there's two other guys in the house."

Just then gunfire erupted from the A-frame: Pop! Pop! Pop! Pop!

Bullets ripped up the ground in front of Fernando and Antonio, who crouched behind Archivada and the other two bodies. While Antonio unlocked his handcuffs and threw them aside, Fernando sighted the two shooters just inside the door. They took turns stepping out in the doorway and firing wildly, then retreating inside to reload their pistols.

Lying flat, Fernando snuggled up against the gorilla with the broken neck. He placed his arm across the dead man's chest and steadied his Smith & Wesson, waiting for one of the shooters to jump out into the open door. Suddenly the dead man's body began to twitch slightly, as if trying to wake up. Another jerk and then the dead man's muscles relaxed. The energy, like air, seemed to drain out of the body once and for all. Leaving just a cadaver, not a person.

Fernando squeezed off a round: Pop!

His bullet shredded the right side of the door frame.

"Fuck this," Antonio said, standing upright and taking aim at the door. When the gorilla on the left side of the door appeared, he and Antonio opened fire at the same time. The gorilla fell backwards. Antonio pitched forward, dropping the gun.

"Are you hit?" Fernando asked.

Antonio held his right hand against his stomach. "Aww, shit," he said and then shook his right hand as if trying to shake out the pain.

Fernando saw the hand was bloodied. He tried to get a close look at the wound.

"It's nothing," Antonio said. "Bullet just nicked my fingers."

"Here," Fernando said, handing Antonio a bandana he always carried in his rear pocket.

Antonio wrapped his hand in the bandana. "It's payback time. I got one more to deal with," he said, motioning toward the A-frame.

Fernando grabbed Antonio by the shoulders. "No, you stay here. Let me do this. You can't use a gun with your hand like that."

Before Antonio could protest, Fernando headed for the A-frame. He crouched low moving off toward the left side of the building. When he reached the front, he stood flat against the logs and shimmied over to the door. He listened for any movement inside but heard nothing. Then he peeked in the door and saw the dead Sinaloa gunman lying on the floor. Beyond the crumpled body the entryway and front room were both empty. No sign of the other shooter.

Moving as quietly as possible, Fernando slipped through the door and fell to one knee, scouring the front room and hallway for any sign of the second shooter, who seemed to have disappeared. Not a trace. So Fernando moved carefully into the long hallway, taking one small step at a time. Now he saw the kitchen in the rear of the building.

Suddenly something crashed in the kitchen. Sounded like pots and pans all hitting the floor at the same time. Fernando froze against the wall.

Then the shooter bolted out of the rear kitchen door. As Fernando watched, the runner stumbled on the porch outside and fell in the dirt. Then he scrambled up and took off running around the back of the A-frame.

"Stop!" Fernando shouted, running outside.

The shooter turned and fired a shot at Fernando: Pop!

The bullet thudded into the logs over Fernando's head. He ducked back inside the kitchen door. Moments later he heard a car engine start. He ran outside and around the A-frame just in time to see the shooter drive off in the Toyota Sequoia. Fernando crouched and tried to steady his aim, but the Sequoia was moving too fast for him to get a good shot. Too late.

Then he saw Lacy. The man in black had walked halfway down the hill overlooking the A-frame. The Grim Reaper himself. Down on one knee, Lacy had a bead on the Sequoia, following it in the scope of his sniper rifle. As the big vehicle entered the clearing near the end of the driveway, a shot rang out in the canyon and echoed loudly: Crack!

Instantly the Sequoia began to swerve to the right. Slowing to a crawl, it rolled off the driveway into a stand of yellow chamisa bushes and came to a stop, engine sputtering.

Lacy stood up, put the SAKO on his shoulder, and continued on down the trail as though nothing out of the ordinary had happened. Just another day at the office. Another kill.

Fernando picked up the handcuffs that Antonio had discarded and then waited for Lacy at the bottom of the trail. "Hell of a shot."

Lacy nodded. "Easy with the SAKO. It's dead accurate up to eleven hundred meters."

"Well, that depends on who's shooting it," Fernando said.

Lacy smiled. "Yes it does."

They walked together across the parking lot to the Sequoia, which had finally stalled when the vehicle came to rest in the bushes. Antonio was already standing there, holding his bleeding hand against his chest. He motioned to the Sequoia. Not a pretty sight. The bullet had shattered the rear window and blown through the driver's neck, almost severing his head from his body. The impact had left him slumped over on the right side of the steering wheel. Blood dripped from the front windshield and dashboard and pooled on the floor mats.

Antonio went to open the driver's door.

"No, don't touch anything," Fernando said. "Police will think this was the work of the Cartel Jalisco. Payback for what the Sinaloa Cartel did to them earlier. Just the ongoing cartel war."

"He's right," Lacy added. "This is exactly what Jalisco would do."

"So we don't talk about this, okay?" Fernando said. "This never happened. We were never here. Agreed?"

Antonio and Lacy nodded.

"Now let's get out of here before the police get here," Fernando said. "Someone must have heard the gunshots and called the police. Jack, I'll drop you off at your BMW. Antonio, I'll take you to Urgent Care to get your hand treated."

The three of them ran back to the Cherokee. Fernando grabbed the abandoned duffle bag and tossed it and the handcuffs in the back of the Cherokee and then waited while Lacy placed his SAKO next to the duffle bag. Then he drove quickly out of the parking lot and down Canyon Road to his former office, where he dropped off Lacy at his BMW.

"Remember, this never happened," Fernando said, waiting while Lacy climbed out of the Cherokee.

"What never happened?" Lacy asked. He stood up stiffly and placed his sniper rifle in its case and then climbed into his BMW.

"Ditto," Antonio said.

After Lacy drove off, Fernando got out of the Cherokee and said, "I'll be right back."

Fernando grabbed the handcuffs he'd picked up at the A-frame and walked behind Essentia, where he tossed the cuffs into an industrial dumpster. Better not to leave any evidence that would suggest the shootout was not related to the cartel war.

Fernando walked back to the Cherokee, now hearing police sirens coming up Canyon Road. Once in the Cherokee, he and Antonio watched two police cruisers speed up the hill toward Upper Canyon Road. As soon as they passed by, Fernando pulled out of the parking lot and headed for the Urgent care on Saint Michael's Drive.

As Fernando turned onto Cerrillos Road, Antonio said, "Yeah...I'll be okay, just take me back to my cabin."

"Let me see your hand," Fernando said.

Antonio held out a bloody kerchief wrapped around mangled fingers.

"You're going straight to Urgent Care," Fernando said.

27

Three days later Fernando had not left his house since the shootout with Sinaloa. He'd decided to lay low, just in case. Meanwhile, he'd occupied himself by going through his computer files one by one, saving the business-related files he needed for possible tax and legal issues and deleting the rest. Tedious work. By the morning of the third day he'd only made it through the last two years. At this rate it would take him days, if not a couple of weeks to complete his cleanup. His eyes tired, Fernando decided to take a break. He closed his laptop and left it on his desk, walking to the kitchen for a third or maybe fourth cup of coffee, he'd lost count.

As he predicted, the shootout on Upper Canyon Road had been reported as a continuation of the war between the Sinaloa and Jalisco cartels. That gave him a good deal of pleasure. So much so that he was having second thoughts about retiring. Why retire now, after he'd just helped rid Santa Fe of two cartels? Not that he was delusional. He knew both cartels would regroup and return in some shape or form, under new leadership. Still, he could set up his office here in his study or in the small storage room in his garage. Wouldn't take much work to set up a home office. That way, he could take on only occasional cases, ones that involved people he knew or that he felt strongly about. Something to consider, even though Estelle would read him the riot act if and when she found out. Could he keep it secret, a secret private eye business that not even his wife knew about?

His cell phone rang just as he was pouring himself the cup of coffee. He saw Antonio's name on the screen. He'd taken Antonio to the Urgent Care facility on Saint Michael's Drive to get his hand bandaged after the shootout on Upper Canyon Road. He would have preferred to take the big man to a real emergency room, but Antonio had categorically refused to set foot inside Christus Saint Vincent Hospital ever again, saying they'd tried to kill him on his last visit. Fernando hadn't argued. You didn't argue with Antonio.

"How's your hand, Antonio?" Fernando answered, taking a seat at the kitchen table.

"Getting better, except I can't chop wood or do much of anything," Antonio said. "I had to ask the son of one of my neighbors down the road to chop wood and bring me groceries. I feel like I'm fucking helpless."

"Well, you need to take it easy for a while," Fernando said. "Don't strain yourself. You have to give the hand time to heal."

"Yeah, I know," Antonio replied, all business. "Listen, I have some news. Jack's leaving town. He says he's tired of Santa Fe and ready to move on."

Fernando smiled. "Hot dog! No kidding? That's the best news I've heard in days."

"I know, I feel the same way, the sooner the better, but here's the thing, he wants to do some touring before he goes," Antonio continued. "He wants to see Dennis Hopper's grave."

"What?" Fernando asked, after a long pause. It took a few moments for Antonio's comment to sink in. "With all the tourist sites in this state, he wants to see Dennis Hopper's grave? No Taos Pueblo or Chaco Canyon? No Museum Hill? Is the man crazy or what?"

"He's a big fan of Hopper, what can I say," Antonio replied. "And to answer your question, he probably is fucking crazy, but at this point I just want to get him out of town, you understand? Send him on his way so he doesn't shoot someone else, someone he shouldn't shoot. Like Dee Highland."

"Copy that," Fernando said. "Anything I can do to expedite his departure, just let me know."

"That's why I'm calling. Can you drive?" Antonio asked. "My hand's still gimpy, and neither of us know where to find Dennis Hopper's grave. Somewhere around Taos, right?"

"Yeah, Jesus Nazareno Cemetery, east of Ranchos de Taos," Fernando said. "I can give you directions."

Antonio sighed. "He doesn't want to drive. I know you're sick of him, but can you do this one more thing, and then we'll be rid of him. Hopefully forever. He wants to visit Hopper's grave this morning and then take the shuttle to the Albuquerque airport tonight. He's returning the BMW he bought to the dealership this afternoon. Ten day grace period."

Fernando didn't respond. He wanted nothing more to do with Lacy, but on the other hand he would like to get Lacy out of town as soon as possible. Make sure Lacy gets on that shuttle to Albuquerque.

"Just one more day," Antonio added. "I know you're sick of him, but what do you say?"

Fernando let loose a few expletives and then said, "Okay, I'll do it, but just to get rid of him. Then I'm done. No more. I never want to hear his name again. You understand?"

"We'll meet you at your house in half an hour," Antonio said and clicked off before Fernando could change his mind or add a few more choice words.

"Half an hour, you must be kidding me," Fernando said to himself, out loud. What was wrong with these people? Half an hour!

Fernando cocked his arm, tempted to throw his cell phone against the kitchen wall, but then thought twice about it and set it down on the table. Just what he needed to start the day, a trip to Jesus Nazareno with Lacy. At least they didn't have to worry about Lacy shooting someone he shouldn't shoot in the cemetery. Everyone there was already dead!

Fernando changed his mind again about retiring. He went back and forth like a damn yoyo. Just when he was thinking of continuing, someone would call and want him to clean up their mess. Now this. Dennis Hopper?

He hadn't been to Jesus Nazareno Cemetery for years, ever since an old friend of his from Taos had died unexpectedly from a massive heart attack. Poor Armando was only 48 when he dropped dead at Michael's Kitchen after eating one last 'widow maker' breakfast of Huevos Rancheros. If he remembered correctly, the cemetery was off State Road 518 not far from San Francisco de Asis, the famous Ranchos de Taos church. Maybe two or three miles east of the church on State Rad 518, the highway into the Carson National Forest. He went into his study and looked for a map in his desk and then in the closets, both of which were stuffed with odds and ends of crap. Halfway through the second closet he remembered he'd taken most, if not all of his New Mexico maps down to his former office on Canyon Road. That meant the maps had been in the box of papers he'd thrown in the dumpster behind Essentia.

He decided to check the storage room in the garage, just in case he'd left one of the maps at home. Too late. When he opened the kitchen door he saw Lacy's blue BMW pulling into his driveway. They must have been parked down the street when Antonio called.

"We're early," Antonio said, jumping out of the BMW.

Lacy took his time getting out of the BMW. No hurry. Dressed in his usual black from head to foot, he sauntered over to the Cherokee and climbed in back, without saying a goddamn word. Antonio joined him, riding shotgun.

Fernando stood on his patio speechless. He didn't like being treated like a fucking chauffeur. If he'd remembered to lock the doors of the Cherokee this wouldn't have happened.

Fernando locked the kitchen door and then climbed into the Cherokee, slamming his door closed.

"You okay?" Antonio asked, noticing Fernando's bad mood.

Fernando didn't respond. He fired up the Cherokee and pulled out on Canyon Road. He took the Paseo to Highway 84/285 and headed northwest past the village of Tesuque and the Santa Fe Opera. Slowing down when he entered the Pojoaque business corridor, he passed the burned-out Line Camp building where Silva Archivada and his Sinaloa gang were fire-bombed. From there it was a straight shot to junky Española, its streets cluttered with fast food joints and small storefront shops The scenery improved once he turned and headed north on Highway 68, otherwise known as the Low Road to Taos.

Meanwhile, Antonio and Lacy talked logistics, how they were going to return Lacy's BMW to the dealer and get him to the Airport Shuttle in time to make his flight at the Albuquerque Sunport. They decided they had to be finished with the BMW paperwork by three o'clock, because the shuttle left for Albuquerque at half past three. That meant Antonio would have to follow him to the dealership and then transport him to the shuttle terminal, injured hand or not. "You can do it," Lacy told Antonio, not showing much sympathy.

Fernando ignored them, still steaming. He wondered how Antonio could give Lacy a ride to the BMW dealership and the shuttle terminal when he couldn't drive to Taos?

Highway 68 ran alongside the Rio Grande as it snaked its way through the river valley. To either side of the river piñon and juniper trees pock-marked the triangular hills. Just past Dixon he began to see brightly colored kayaks and white water rafts bobbing and splashing their way down the river. Approaching the parking areas near Pilar he saw trailers belonging to the commercial rafting companies parked side by side on the gravel lots. Several rafts were in the process of launching. Two rafters wearing orange life jackets and helmets waved at him as he drove by on the highway. The colorful scene perked up Fernando's mood a bit. At least he could enjoy the scenery.

Fernando drove around the last sweeping curve and then up the hill to the Taos plateau and into the community of Ranchos de Taos. He slowed down driving past the famous San Francisco de Asis church, painted and photographed by Georgia O'Keeffe and a zillion other artists. And more to the point for the three of them today, where Dennis Hopper's funeral had taken place back in 2010. Ahead the ribbon of highway ran straight to the 13,000-foot Taos Mountains on the far horizon. Would be nice, as he knew from previous hiking and camping trips, but they were going to

Jesus Nazareno Cemetery to visit Dennis Hopper's grave. Go figure.

Fernando turned right onto Highway 518 and drove down the old two-lane highway. Minutes later he turned left into the unpaved parking lot of Jesus Nazareno Cemetery. Surrounded by a wire fence, Jesus Nazareno was overrun by weeds and colorful wildflowers, a tumbledown collection of stone markers and hand-carved wooden crosses, backgrounded by the deep blue Taos mountains to the north and west. It was so untended and *au naturel*, not to mention starkly beautiful, that it took your breath away. Fernando had been here before, Lacy and Antonio hadn't. The three of them sat in the Cherokee staring at the cemetery. None of them said a word. They sat in silence, spellbound.

"Well," Fernando said after a time. "Are you getting out or what? This is where Hopper is buried. I can show you his grave." With that Fernando climbed out of the Cherokee and stretched his cramping muscles. The fresh mountain air invigorated him, as it always did. He waited for Antonio.

Antonio grumbled as he squeezed his six-foot-eight, 280-pound body out of the Cherokee. "I hate cemeteries, I don't care how beautiful they are."

"You should see the Truchas cemeteries, they're even more beautiful," Fernando said.

They turned around, thinking Lacy would follow, but the man in black remained in the back seat, clutching the seat in front of him. Frozen. As though he'd suffered a stroke.

They waited impatiently for him, but Lacy didn't move.

28

"Is he getting out of the car or what?" Fernando asked a few minutes later, when Lacy still hadn't moved.

Antonio threw open his hands. "I don't know what the problem is," he said, disgusted. Then he turned and walked over to the cemetery. The bandage on his right hand had started to unravel. When he walked, he trailed a foot-long length of tape that flapped against his huge leg.

Fernando followed Antonio, ignoring Lacy. They walked through the fence on a dirt path, free from weeds. Off to their right they passed by a wooden ramada under which a statue of Jesus knelt on the ground struggling with his heavy wooden cross. Jesus wore a crown of thorns, with streaks of blood sliding down his delicately painted face, flesh-colored with a black beard and dark, penetrating eyes. Blue and white flowers, real and artificial, were scattered around the statue. Someone had been here recently bringing flowers.

Fernando looked back at Lacy, who still hadn't moved. "Why isn't Lacy coming? This was his idea, right?"

Antonio shrugged. "He says the dead make him uneasy."

Taken aback, Fernando said, "That's ironic, since he makes his living off the dead. Making people dead, that is!"

"I guess, but maybe it's just the price he pays," Antonio responded.

Fernando studied Antonio, unsure of what the big man meant. The more he thought about it, the less he wanted to think about it. Disturbing undercurrents. The psychology of it all troubled him. "Then why did he insist on coming here if he's uncomfortable?"

"He has a thing for Dennis Hopper," Antonio explained. "Jack said he met Hopper once in L.A. after he came back from Iraq and that Hopper gave him some good advice. About what, I don't know."

Just then they heard a car door open and close. Then they saw Lacy come shuffling down the dirt path. His eyes were fixed straight ahead, avoiding the statue of Jesus with his cross. He looked harried, bedeviled, as though he had a swarm of bats flapping around his head.

"This way," Fernando said, leading them halfway down the path to Dennis Hopper's grave, where a beautifully carved wooden cross had been erected on a mound of dirt and rock. Headbands and scarves of all colors had been placed on the wooden cross by Hopper's fans, remembering the actor's role in his most famous movie, *Easy Rider*, parts of it filmed nearby in Taos, where Hopper lived at the time. Several people had brought bouquets of bright flowers and someone had tucked a leather pouch into an American flag placed next to the wooden cross. An empty whiskey bottle, two full cans of Coors beer, and several joints completed the graveside décor. Seemed perfect for Hopper.

Lacy stopped a good ten yards away and stood staring at the grave, as if afraid to come closer. The words engraved in the wooden cross read: "Dennis Lee Hopper, Born 5-17-36, Died 5-29-10."

Fernando and Antonio stood behind Lacy waiting impatiently for whatever Lacy wanted to do or say to mark the occasion.

Several minutes passed before Lacy spoke. "I met Dennis once at a club in L.A. after I returned from Iraq. We'd been drinking all afternoon. He was wild and free and talked nonstop about whatever popped into his mind. Me, I was lost and confused, not understanding the hostility I felt from most people after coming back from the war. I was alienated from my own county. I'll never forget what he told me that afternoon: 'Fuck it! You don't owe your country anything. They turned you into an assassin. That's your country now.'"

"Are you okay?" Fernando asked, noticing Lacy's agitation and worried that he was about to come unhinged.

Lacy made a face. He stretched out his arms as if embracing the entire cemetery, all of the dead. "I'm one of them. I died in Iraq. Maybe not physically, but spiritually or whatever you want to call it. I can feel them, their turbulence. I'm on their same frequency. I'm dead inside."

Hearing that, Fernando moved away from Lacy, frightened by Lacy's vision. Not many things had frightened Fernando over the past sixty years as much as Lacy frightened him now. He turned away from Lacy and looked west past the scattered wooden crosses to the deep blue Taos Mountains silhouetted against the light blue New Mexico sky, a vision of eternity a la Georgia O'Keeffe.

With that, Lacy started walking back to the Cherokee, shoulders slumped. He did not look back.

Fernando and Antonio watched Lacy walk out of the cemetery and climb into the Cherokee.

"Dead inside?" Fernando asked. "Like them?"

Antonio threw up his hands. "He's decided to go back to Europe, Copenhagen or Amsterdam maybe, one of those new and modern cities where he doesn't know anyone and no one knows him. He needs to keep moving."

"He'll never outrun the ghosts," Fernando said.

Antonio nodded. "Maybe not, but he has to keep running."

Smiling, Fernando kicked at the dirt and said, "Well, let's get him on that plane. Then I can finally retire."

"Promises, promises," Antonio replied.

Readers Guide

1. Who is Jack Lacy and why are the Santa Fe Police worried about his appearance in Santa Fe?

2. How and from whom do we learn about why Lacy has come to Santa Fe?

3. What is Sargent Antonio Blake's connection to Lacy? How does he feel about Lacy's arrival in Santa Fe?

4. Why has Lacy come to Santa Fe?

5. What prevents Lacy from carrying out his 'hit'?

6. What causes the bloody war that develops between Lacy and Silva Archivada, the head of the Sinaloa Cartel in New Mexico? How does Private Investigator Fernando Lopez get drawn into the war between Lacy and the Sinaloa Cartel?

7. Lopez and Blake discover at the La Fonda Hotel that Lacy sees and is afraid of Ghosts. Why? Explain.

8. How do Lacy and Lopez defeat the Sinaloa Cartel gunmen and get Antonio back safely?

9. Early on Lopez learns that a second Mexican cartel has begun operating in Santa Fe, the Cartel Jalisco Nueva Generacion. How does this cartel figure prominently in Lacy and Lopez's plans to cover up their role in defeating the Sinaloa Cartel?

10. Why does Lacy want to visit Dennis Hopper's grave at Jesus Nazareno Cemetery in Ranchos de Taos?

11. In the final scene at the cemetery, Lacy reflects on his obsession with the dead and with the ghosts he sees regularly. Why is he obsessed? What is Lopez's reaction to all this?

READERS GUIDE

1. Who is Jacob Lacy and why are the Santa Fe Police worried about his appearance in Santa Fe?

2. How and from whom do we learn about why Lacy resigned as Santa Fe ...?

3. What is Sargent Antonio Blaze's connection to Lacy? How does he feel about Lacy's arrival in Santa Fe?

4. Why has Lacy come to Santa Fe?

5. What prevents Lacy from carrying out his turf?

6. What causes the bloody war that develops between Lacy and Silva Arbulido, the head of the Sinaloa Cartel in New Mexico? How does Ferrara, a former Federal prosecutor, get drawn into the war between Lacy and the Sinaloa Cartel?

7. Lopez and Blaze discover at the Hacienda Hotel that Lacy was not being straight. Why? Explain.

8. How do Lacy and Lopez defeat the Sinaloa Cartel gunmen and get Antonio back safely?

9. Kanyon Lopez learns that a second Mexican cartel has begun operating in Santa Fe, the Cartel Jalisco Nueva Generacion. How does this cartel figure prominently in Lacy and Lopez's plans to cover up their role in defeating the Sinaloa Cartel?

10. Why did Lacy want to visit Delilah Lopez's grave at Jesus Nazareno Cemetery in Albuquerque?

11. In the final scene of the cemetery, Lacy reflects on the obsession with the dead and would be ghosts he sees regularly. What is he obsessed? What connects them all?